THE COLD CA

I am a local writer self-publishing my books on Amazon.

If you like this and would like to read more my books are available @ Amazon Books.

Or contact me directly via Facebook.

            Enjoy.

JAMES GLACHAN

CASE 1.

Colin Fisher, murdered. 4th June, 2000.

Crosshouse, East Ayrshire

ONE

JOHN ROSE noticed a different atmosphere in the detective's room but thought it was because most were back on the Tuesday after being off the weekend for Easter.

No, it was more than that. Something was up. Nobody was affording him eye contact. Not that he had much respect for most of the other guys. Oh, and ladies, if you could call the 2 female detectives that.

He buttonholed Amy Hammond who was walking past with a mug of coffee and trying to subtly ignore him.

'Hi Amy. Good weekend?'

'I was on. Serious assault in Ardrossan on Saturday.'

Boy, could he pick the wrong person to ask, he thought.

'Oh, have you met your new boss?' she asked, a faint smirk played on her lips for a second but long enough for John to notice.

'New boss?'

'Here he is now,' she added, looking over his shoulder as she said it.

John turned on his heels and his heart sank. His new boss was one of the new breed; graduates who were quickly pushed through the ranks to positions miles above their ability.

'You must be Detective Sergeant John Rose, Detective Inspector Kevin Walker,' he said, extending his hand. 'Pleased to meet you.'

John thought he could judge a man by his handshake. Walker's was limp and felt soft and warm to the touch. It was the limp bit he felt would prove right in the future.

John's in comparison was firm and masculine and he felt like squeezing his new boss's until it hurt but didn't want to get off on the wrong foot, so to speak.

'Heard a lot of good stuff about you.'

Before John could say anything Walker continued.

'I have a nice wee job I think will be right up your street. Come on up to my office.'

John followed his new boss with growing dread. What he reckoned might be up his street worried him more with every step.

'Where did D.I. Hannah go?'

'Oh, she was head hunted to Govan. Left quickly which was why I only arrived at short notice on Friday.'

John shook his head. Victoria Hannah was hopeless, how bad did you have to be to get a job at headquarters, he thought to himself.

'Please sit,' the D.I. said as they went into his office.

Looking round John and found everything anally neat. Seemed to sum the guy up in John's mind.

'John,' he started after taking his seat behind his desk. 'We are trying a new initiative here in Saltcoats. Each division is starting a new independent cold case department covering the whole of Ayrshire and we want you to head it up.'

'Head it up, eh. How many are in this new department?'

'Well, to start with, just you. I can't spare any detectives at the moment, unless you want somebody from uniform to help you, I can arrange that.'

'No thanks,' John said more enthusiastically than maybe he should have.

The reality was sinking in fast; he was being pushed out of the detective pool and this new guy was getting the job of doing the pushing. Poor shmuck would have been sold him on the new "initiative" and being new to the station didn't know the politics there yet.

It was no surprise to John, he knew he was regarded by his bosses as a bit of a troublemaker as well as a rebel just because he stuck his head above the parapet and moaned through lockdown about insufficient manning, excessive hours worked and just about anything else he didn't agree with while all the other detectives put up and shut up. Plus, the fact was he used his own methods not in the detective's code book if there was such a tome.

'So, where is this new department going to be situated?'

'IT have set up an office for you upstairs.'

John reckoned that must be a new record for the IT department to be that quick with anything. There again, this might have been planned for weeks.

There was a keyring on Walker's desk with a single key on it, which Kevin started to finger gently. Next to it was an old manilla folder.

The D.I. picked up the folder.

'This is the first case we want you to look over.'

He handed the folder over and John started reading the front cover.

'A young lad called Colin Fisher who was only 18 when he was murdered,' the D.I. said.

John had already established that, he had opened the front and was skim reading the first page.

'Crosshouse? Not exactly local, is it?'

'We are Scottish Police now, and we are Ayrshire division. As I said earlier we are covering cold cases that cover the whole of Ayrshire.

There are 2 things here. Firstly, it was thought a fresh pair of eyes looking over the case could get results and secondly it would have been his 40th birthday on the 3rd of next month and the newspapers are going to do a big feature on the case.

Top brass wants the public to know every unsolved case is never closed.'

John stopped reading and looked up at his boss.

'That's just over 3 weeks from now. It's not a detective you need, it's a miracle worker.'

Walker gave him a smug look. 'That's why you were chosen, John.'

John just shook his head, while the phrase "patronising prick" came to his mind.

John followed his new boss up the stairs to his new office. Walker almost ceremoniously opened the office door, switched on the light then handed John the key.

John went in and sat behind the desk, sitting the folder in front of him. Before he started reading it further he realised he needed his essentials from his old desk.

John left the office with the key and suddenly a spring in his step. The thought of working on his own brought a smile to his face. He didn't have much time for his fellow officers. They were all younger and fixed in their ideas. Although not exactly a rebel John's methods were dated, most of his fellow detectives thought of him as some sort of dinosaur but the most important thing was- he got results.

As he emptied his desk nobody in the room acknowledged him or even looked in his direction. Suddenly, all were busy on their computers or phones. Not that it bothered him.

His belongings fitted into his work bag, a small holdall that had only contained his sandwiches when he walked into the station that morning but ended bulging to the seams with all the bits and pieces essential for crime solving. Most importantly, his mug and teaspoon.

Walking up the stairs, the noise of his footsteps echoed in the well. He looked down at the keyring, room 2/28 it had been labelled. For all the times he had been there he was sure he had never been in there before.

When he re-opened the door he saw, apart from the desk and chair with his computer on it, there were a couple of filing cabinets, that turned out to be empty and on the opposite wall were shelves, stacked with boxes. Obviously the files for his new case, the boy Fisher's murder.

No wonder he hadn't been in there before, it was a cupboard. They hadn't even disguised it by removing the marks on the walls where the shelves had been against the walls.

Still, John couldn't wait to get going and started reading the folder his boss had given him before even switching on his computer.

The case notes intrigued him so much before he knew it 12 o'clock was upon him. He had worked through his tea break which he always had at just after 10. It was only the rumbling in his stomach that had him looking at his watch.

Switching on his computer he headed off to make a cuppa while it booted up. As he ate his sandwiches he googled Colin Fisher murder.

Page after page appeared. The local paper had most of the reports and the one that caught his interest was one from the 10th anniversary of Colin's murder from 2010.

It focussed on an interview of Calum Hunter who had been with Colin on the fateful night. After playing football in the afternoon, they headed for the dancing in Ayr on the Saturday night. They shared a taxi home and just after leaving the cab Colin took a short cut through the park. That was the last time he saw him alive.

'I want a wee word with you,' John said to the computer screen as he pointed to the image of Calum Hunter from a shot of the local paper.

John added some notes from the article in his A5 notebook. He always carried one with him and wrote copious notes in it.

On the whiteboard on the wall, he wrote his usual starting headings: who, when, where, with what, why and who did it.

WHO: Colin Fisher, aged 18, heading home from the dancing.

WHEN: Sunday 4th June 2000.

WHERE: Entrance to the playing fields, Crosshouse, from Hunter Street.

WITH WHAT? Unknown.

WHY and WHO DID IT remained unpopulated.

He also noted some other notes:

Did not seem to be a robbery, his wallet found near his body with money and his cards in it.

Taxi driver was foreign. Looked like Tony Blair.

John checked the crime scene pictures of the body and had a good idea of where the body was found and that was where he was going after his lunch, to see the crime scene. Pictures only told you so much, he thought.

TWO

John parked his car at the entrance to the playing fields in Hunter Street. He had driven to the end of the cul-de-sac and noted where the path through was on the way past before turning and heading back down to park. He stopped just before the pathway to the park.

Getting out of the car he noticed how quiet the street was, even for the middle of the day.

Crosshouse was about 15 miles from his base in Saltcoats Police station and he had taken about 25 miles to drive there. He relaxed his stiff muscles before moving off.

Arriving at around 1:30 he found the park empty safe for a woman walking 2 dogs, away at the far end of the park. It was so quiet, deadly quiet in fact, save for the odd barking from the dogs as the woman had them chasing balls.

John walked down the tarmacked path to where the stricken body lay. Out of reverence, he stood next to where he imagined the body had been found but not on the very spot. Looking up again he wondered if the current park users knew it's gristly past. Probably too young.

John was disturbed by an ancient Jack Russell sniffing at his ankle and shoe.

The owner of the dog, who had walked down behind him, seemed as ancient as his mutt.

'Sorry about him son. He's got cataracts and lumbago.'

John smiled; he hadn't heard the word lumbago since he read the Broon's in the Sunday Post when he was a boy.

'Are you from the council?' the old man continued. 'We need bigger bins in the park here. Look, they are overflowing again.'

The old guy probably thought he worked for the council because John always wore a suit and shirt and tie to work. It hadn't been required for years but John thought a smart look gave an impression of competence.

Just yards away from them was a litter bin filled to overflowing and he saw what the old guy's issue was. Small black bags of dog's doings and empty plastic water bottles were scattered at the base.

'They have games here at the weekend and the bins are filled then your lot don't empty them until a Wednesday. I have to take wee Hector's doings home and put them in our green bin. In the hot weather the bins stink of shit.'

'I'm not with the council, sir.'

The old guy and his mutt shuffled away a few yards then stopped suddenly when the old man had a thought and turned and shuffled back towards him.

'You are the Police, aren't you.'

For a second John felt like saying "elementary my dear Watson" on a whim, but decided against the smart-ass comments, this guy could be a help.

'Yes, sir. Detective Sergeant John Rose. And you are?'

'Hamish Hamilton,' he said as he gave a sort of salute.

'This is about the young lad that was murdered all those years ago, isn't it?' he continued.

'Yes. I rework cold cases.'

'Och, we have had folk round every few years digging things up again. You do know how much it just upsets folk, brings back terrible memories for his parents and everybody involved. It's not right.'

'Surely they still want closure. Somebody killed their son, and the guilty party has gotten away with it for all these years.'

The guy looked up and had tears in his eyes which he wiped at with his hand.

'I found the body that Sunday morning. Thought he was just drunk but when I leaned down to check he was stone cold. Then, when I saw the wound on the back of his head, I knew he was dead.'

John patted the old man's back reassuringly.

'Must have been terrible. So where is it you live?'

The old man pointed over the large hedge that provided a boundary along the side of the park.

'The second house along.'

'Did you hear anything the previous night?'

'Yes, we heard shouting just after midnight. Thought it was just folk heading home from the pub. Just some shouting. It wasn't unusual, folk come through the park coming home from the pub. Anyway, we have told this to so many Police over the years.'

The old man paused, then added, 'always wondered if it would have been different if I got up and went out that night.'

The old man's shoulders drooped. 'Better let Hector do his business.'

With that he turned and shuffled back down the path while Hector ambled along the grass, sniffing as he went.

John watched as he went and waited for the 5 minutes or so as old Hector deposited what it had to, and the old man dutifully picked it up and deposited it in a pooh bag.

The old guy must have felt rebellious because he just dropped the dog's pooh bag beneath the bin beside the others deposited there.

As Hamish reached John again the policeman stopped him.

'Do you mind if we go back to your place, and I ask you a few more questions?'

The old guy raised the hand that wasn't holding the dog's leash.

'Why? You must have it all on record.'

'Not the questions I will ask you. I work differently from other detectives.'

'Okay, then. If you think it will help.'

The old man's bungalow was neat and tidy. When he unleashed Hector he went straight to his basket in the lounge and quickly got curled up in it.

'It's a dog's life, eh,' John said.

'Take a seat. Well, what do you want to know?'

'What do you know about what happened that night?'

'Well, it's going back a bit, but I will see what I can remember. The lads got a taxi from the dancing in Ayr. Colin went down the lane and somebody whacked him. That's about as much as I remember.

What I can tell you is the atmosphere in the estate wasn't right for a long, long while after that, thinking there was a killer amongst us.'

'I can imagine.'

'Can you son? Can you really? Suddenly all your neighbours are suspects, there is nobody you can trust anymore. Can you really imagine that son?'

Hamish had turned to look John in the eye.

'No, I suppose not. So, who were the other lads?'

'Adam Hunter's boy. Nice boy, he is an electrician. Moved away to Paisley way I think. Hughy McDowall's boy was there. I can't remember his name. He moved somewhere on the coast, might have been Largs or Fairlie. Somewhere posh.'

The old guy paused for a breath.

'Was there not 4 of them?'

The old man nodded.

'Young Davy Hood was the other one. He went right off the rails after that. Drugs and drink then he took to stealing to pay for his habit. Good footballer when he was young. At one time Ayr United wanted to sign him.'

'Couldn't have been that good,' John said quietly to himself.

'When he was bad his father Davy Senior covered for him but couldn't stop him doing drugs and stuff. Far as I know the boy is an alcoholic now, you see him stoating about the town. Bloody shame.'

'Do the parents still all live in the town?'

'Village son. We call Crosshouse a village. Davy senior passed away last year. They said it was Covid, but many say it was from a broken heart after the way his lad turned out. The rest of the parents are still here in the village. Three of them live in the Varney here. The Fishers live in Irvine Road.'

'The Varney. Is that what this estate is called.'

'Yes. Everybody calls it the Varney. That was the mob that built the place and the name stuck.'

'Okay, Hamish, thanks for your help.'

'Help? How did I help?'

'Well, like I said, I work differently. Too many people listen without hearing. Oh, by the way, could you tell me where young Davy Hood and his mother live now?'

'He's back living with his mum. She lives in Dean Avenue I think.'

'Right, thanks again. I will see myself out.

John put Dean Avenue in his Satnav and headed round the street to find the address. The avenue was only a small street of a dozen or so bungalows. His plan was just to scope the area for now, knocking doors would come later.

THREE

Next morning John dressed casually and got the bus from his home in Irvine to Crosshouse. Getting off at the church, in the middle of the town, he walked back along Irvine Road heading toward the shops.

Everybody he passed wished him good morning. Obviously his casual gear disguised his occupation which rarely got him any smiles or spontaneous salutations.

After he made it back to the centre of the village he headed up towards the Varney estate. He had only walked about a hundred yards when it looked like his intended target appeared walking towards him.

Why he thought it was Davy Hood walking towards him he didn't know, maybe his Police intuition?

John checked his watch, just before 10 o'clock. Davy Hood was heading to the local Spar for a carry-out, the cop was certain of that.

Trying to look casual John walked back to the bench just down from the drink shop.

The guy approached, head down, walking slowly towards the shop.

John thought he looked a right state. His face was blotchy, red sores broken out, his lips cracked and sore looking and his tousled hair obviously hadn't seen a comb that morning. Maybe a few other mornings too.

'Davy, is that you?'

He turned with bloodshot eyes and looked unknowingly.

'Jim Smith. Our Liam played with you at football when you were kids.'

It was almost sore for John to watch Davy trying to remember the boy Liam, who he had he played football with him over 20 years previously. Especially when the lad didn't exist.

'How are you doing, Davy?'

'I am doing all right, man. How's Liam?'

'He is doing okay. He's married and lives up near Aberdeen. Never see him now.'

Davy sat down on the bench next to John.

'Is he coming down for the game on Sunday?'

'The game?'

'Charity game in memory of Fishy. We are playing the current team.'

'Fishy. Oh, Colin Fisher. Sad that. Such a nice boy. He could have played senior, same as yourself. I always thought that.'

'He didn't take football seriously, he just wanted to play with us, his pals in the amateurs. Fun on the park then the boozer before the dancing, that was what he liked. It was his dad that always pushed him.

Think his dad was jealous because I could have gone senior.'

'What happened that night? You were with him, weren't you.'

Davy went quiet for a minute. John thought as the silence went on that he was going to open up to him about what happened that night and give him the breakthrough he wanted.

Davy turned and stared at him before getting up. There was bitterness in his eyes.

'I don't know who you are, but I never played with a Liam Smith or a Liam anybody. What are you Police or reporter? Never mind, one is as bad as the other.'

With that he got up and started to walk towards the off-licence before turning and pointing to the copper.

'Don't come near me again or you will be sorry.'

Then he spat in his direction, but his aim was way short of it's target.

John waited until he disappeared into the shop before getting up. Davy had been a blowout but if the team was playing on the Sunday it would be a chance to see the lads together and maybe get to speak to some more locals.

Over at the shop window there was a poster in the window advertising the charity match on the Sunday with a 2 o'clock kick off.

John got the bus back to Irvine, where he lived, arriving in time for lunch with his wife, Karen.

Tomato soup and crusty bread was one of his favourites, taking him back to being a kid, sitting with his mum in front of the telly watching cartoons.

Instead of being in front of the telly they sat at the kitchen table.

'How did it go today?'

Karen and John had been married for nearly 40 years, through 3 houses and 4 changes of job. The last 22 years he had been in the Police, being allowed to join when they raised the age of joining to 40 to get more experienced people in the force.

Over his time there Karen didn't often ask what he was working on, but his change of work routine obviously intrigued her. After all, after all those years of wearing uniform then suited and booted to suddenly going dressed casually and on the bus was definitely a diversion.

'Didn't go as well as I hoped but I have a positive lead. I will need to work on Sunday. If they will let me.'

'Sunday? You are going to work overtime?'

'No, I will take it as time in lieu.'

'Doing what?'

'Right, what I can tell you is I am working a cold case. An 18-year-old lad was murdered in Crosshouse 22 years ago. His mates are having a charity football match on Sunday, and I want to police it, mingle with them and see what I can pick up from the folk.'

'What, are there no suspects?'

'Nothing at all according to the case book. He was at the dancing with his mates in Ayr. After they got out of the taxi he took a short-cut through the park and was attacked. Nobody saw or heard anything and as far as the notes I have read so far there are no suspects.

When I go back this afternoon I am going to read through some more of the evidence but there are tons of it.'

'What if they did a runner?'

'What?'

'You know, all got out of the taxi and run off and not pay. Maybe the driver chased them, and he was the unlucky one. You told me you did that once.'

Although cringing with embarrassment at the thought of something he did, only once, when he was about the lads ages, it might not be right, but John suddenly thought it might just be a eureka moment.

John quickly processed the possible scenario: what if the lads had tried to run and the driver chased them maybe he caught up with Colin. The driver had maybe been caught by this before and decided on retribution but accidentally hit him on the head.

'Karen, love, you might be a genius.'

'What do you mean might be?'

'Well, it's only a theory now. If it turns out to be right then you will be a genius.

FOUR

John parked his own car in the public car park at the village centre. He was dressed in his P.C. uniform as he was playing the part of village bobby that day, while he patrolled the park while the charity game was on.

The uniform was only 2 years old. He had ordered a new one because his old one didn't fit, too tight in too many places. A combination of middle-aged spread and irregular hours disturbing his eating pattern.

He also got it because at the back of his mind he always had a feeling his bosses would bust him back to street cop in order to get him to retire. That hadn't happened but only because he was good at his job. Detective work can be learned but some people, like him, just had a knack for it.

The park was busy when he reached it. There was an ice cream van and a burger stall, and both were doing good business.

Both teams were on the pitch warming up, the contrast easy to see. The younger, fitter guys were going through a strenuous warm-up, the older heads strolling and knocking a ball about. Many holding a can of beer or smoking a ciggie as they did so.

John headed for the changing rooms and knocked gently on the referee's changing room.

'Come!' he heard from within.

When he walked in the referee was in the middle of changing. He had his black shorts and socks on and a string vest. He looked shocked at the Policeman in front of him.

'Is something wrong?'

'No. I was just wondering if you had team lines. Do you need them for a charity match?'

'Yes. The amateur association are sticklers for shit like that.'

The official handed the 2 bits of paper. The paper resembled the teams, the young team's sheet neat and tidy and printed on official paper, the old mob's crumbled and nearer to a scribble than print on a blank sheet.

John took his notebook out. It was a small book, his usual A5 didn't fit in his uniform pockets.

He quickly scanned the old boy's list and took note, Calum Hunter was No.5, Isaac McDowall No.11.

'Wow,' he said when he saw Davy Hood was listed as No.13. He couldn't be playing, he thought, not when he saw the state of him the other day. Probably be going to make a token appearance if anything, he thought.

'Thanks ref. This should be a stroll in the park, charity match.'

The ref, who was, John guessed, in his late 50's and judging from the age and style of his ref gear had been blowing the whistle for many years.

'You would think so. That's why I wondered why you were here, I thought it had kicked off already.'

'Maybe my presence will prevent anything kicking off.'

The referee laughed. 'Right, okay,' he said before pulling on his black top.

The game kicked off to a great cheer from the couple of hundred folk on the side lines. The amateur team wore their all-red home strip, the Old Crocks, as they were listed as, wore the away strip of all white.

Straight away the reds took control, knocking the ball about leaving the crocks more like statues. In fact, there seemed to be more of them than the whites.

The ball was played out to the wing and the No.7 for the lads took the ball in his stride and sped down toward the goal line. The nearest crock lunged in and sent the young lad into the air, screaming as he went.

The referee's shrill whistle blew enthusiastically. Several blasts to show he realised the severity of the tackle. He ran over to the stricken player to check if he was injured or not.

Seeing he was okay he turned his attention to the other players, looking for somebody. He blew his whistle again before calling out.

'Captain!' he roared and pointed in the direction of the crock's team.

A large lump of a guy ambled over, innocent as a choirboy.

John was near enough on the touchline to hear the conversation.

'Look, the game is 1 minute old, and that tackle was terrible. Remember why we are here. This is a charity game!'

The ref said it a bit theatrically loudly for the benefit of the side lines.

The big guy put a hand up, acknowledging, then turned to his players.

'You heard the man,' he said to his teammates then walked back into position. 'Don't kick them until I tell you to.'

This got a laugh from the crowd and lightened the moment.

As he turned and walked away John saw the big guy was wearing the No.5 jersey, the captain was none other than Calum Hunter.

The rest of the half was played in better spirit and when the ref blew for half-time the score was sitting at Amateurs 2 Crocks 1.

John spent most of the first half circulating through the crowd. One guy had asked why he was there, were the Police expecting trouble? He said he was just doing a bit of Community Policing. After all they knew why they were there, the Police hadn't forgotten either.

With about 20 minutes left there was a buzz going through the crowd.

John looked round to see if he could find the source and saw attention was focused on a new sub walking over from the changing rooms.

It was Davy Hood. Walking slowly towards his teammates on the touchline. John walked over in that direction to try and hear what was being said.

Calum Hunter was off the park now and had been barking instructions to the team on the park.

John reached the Crocks camp in time to hear Calum tell Davy to roll back the years. They needed 2 goals to win, that was all.

John was surprised to see how good Davy looked after witnessing him a few days previously. He was clean shaven, and his hair tidily combed and still wet as if he was just out of the shower.

The ref was called over, and Davy took to the park to a chorus of cheers from all round the park.

As he jogged slowly on Calum shouted after him, 'do it for Colin.'

Davy gave a thumbs up and headed toward the opposing goal.

The Crocks had to weather another storm as the youngsters tried to increase their lead. When it broke down a huge diagonal ball found the Crocks No.11, Isaac MacDowall, in acres of space.

He rolled back the years and sprinted with the ball to the goal-line and crossed into the box where Davy Hood rose majestically and headed the ball unstoppably into the opposing net.

The place erupted as the goal was pure quality added to the fact one of their old heroes was back.

While the Crocks celebrated Davy was still on the ground, not even trying to get up. Suddenly there was concern and players from both teams ran to his aid.

When he was helped back to his feet he raised his hands in the air and the crowd cheered again.

With the match drawn again there was suddenly an edge to it. Everybody was playing for pride now, nobody wanted to lose.

Time after time play was stopped for niggly fouls. The ferocity of each tackle gaining momentum until when Isaac McDowall broke into the opposing box seeming certain to score when he was scythed down from behind, suddenly causing a mass brawl on the pitch.

The referee ran up and was blowing his whistle madly, but nobody paid heed. It seemed as though every player on the pitch was facing up to his opponent.

One by one heads in the crowd were turning in towards John, looking, no doubt for his intervention.

When punches were thrown the policeman knew it was time to act. He had been standing at the rear of the crowd and had to push through to get pitch-side. As he ran onto the pitch somebody must have flicked a foot out and tripped him, sending him sprawling onto the pitch and landing flat on his face.

There was uproar as those in the crowd nearest John, who witnessed him go down, burst out laughing. The laughter spread round the pitch and soon onto the pitch itself as the fighting stopped and the laughing began.

John got up slowly and looked across at the mass of players now pointing and laughing. All he could do was take a bow then walk sheepishly back off the park.

As he was leaving the field of play he looked at the guys standing either side of where he had gone onto the pitch, but both looked innocently at him.

Meanwhile a gang of about 20 local neds had started loudly shouting- 'P.C. Plod, he fell over,' over and over while some of the others in the crowd joined in.

John, who wished the ground had swallowed him up when he fell onto the pitch, could only wave over and acknowledge them.

They roared in response and gave up the chant.

On the park the players were set for the penalty for the Crocks that the ref had given when McDowall was brought down.

Standing over the ball was Davy Hood who ran a hand through his hair. He stepped back. There was silence all around as the crowd seemed to collectively hold it's breath.

Just as he went to stride forward a call came from somewhere in the crowd.

'Miss junkie!'

Calum Hunter, who was back on the pitch by then, took a step back from the players lined along the edge of the penalty area and pointed to the area where the call came from.

'One more crack and the smart ass with the big mouth will be visiting his dentist tomorrow for dentures.'

This bought a laugh from the crowd then it went quiet again.

The referee blew his whistle again and Davy took a small step back.

'He must be shitting himself,' somebody on the touchline close to John said in little more than a whisper.

Davy took 2 steps back, strode forward and crashed the ball into the net, past the despairing keeper who managed to get a hand to the ball, but the ferociousness of the hit meant he couldn't stop it.

A cheer went up then the referee blew his whistle repeatedly, signalling the end of the game.

Peace on the park had now been restored and there were handshakes all round.

John watched as the crowd started to disperse. Although he had seen the other 2 guys that had been with Colin and Davy on the fateful night he would really like to have a word with them.

He walked toward the changing ends when he was approached by a large white-headed gent wearing the clubs rain jacket, obviously a team official.

'Officer, are you coming over to the community centre. There's a wee purvey on.'

'Why, do you think there will be trouble?'

The fat man laughed, as if it was the funniest thing he had ever heard.

'No, no, it was nice of you to come out today.'

'The truth is, I have an ulterior motive. I am looking into Colin's murder and hoped to have a word with a few folk here.'

The look on the old guy's face couldn't hide the fact he wished he hadn't just invited John.

John ignored it, he had a job to do, no matter what folk thought of him.

'Where is the community centre?'

'Eh, just down from the car park. You will see most of the folk heading over there.'

John headed back to his car and left the stab vest and his tie in the boot and put his casual jacket on.

FIVE

John walked into the hall and was hit by the aroma of baking. He didn't think he was hungry, but the smell suddenly made his belly rumble.

However, before he could even seek out the food he was accosted by a raffle ticket seller.

John pulled out a £20 note.

'How many?'

'Twenty pounds worth.'

The wee woman looked aghast and looked round for her friend who was across the hall selling her share of tickets.

'Agnes, come here when you have a minute.'

Then she looked at John as she expertly ripped pages from her book of raffles to explain why she called Agnes over.

'You will be better with 10 sheets from the 2 different books.'

Agnes made her way over and started ripping out tickets when her friend explained why she called her over.

'You are the policeman. You already put a tenner in the collection tub,' Agnes said, when she recognised John out of his uniform.

'It's for a good cause,' John said, although he didn't know who or what the monies raised would benefit.

John walked over and joined the buffet queue just as the players started to arrive, obviously delayed by changing and showering.

The younger players came in 1st and formed a guard of honour for the winning Crocks team.

As they filed in everybody applauded them. The greatest cheer reserved for Davy Hood and Calum Hunter, who were last 2 to walk in.

Davy raised a hand and acknowledged them while Calum waved them to stop clapping. When he had quietened them and had their attention he shouted simply, 'let's get pissed!'

This got a laugh and a cheer and had all the players heading for the bar to do as they were told.

John grabbed a plate of food then found a seat on his own, as far away from the crowd as he could so that he could observe the goings on and wait for his chance to speak to Calum and Isaac. Maybe even have a word with Davy.

As the afternoon passed there was a steady trail of people heading outside for a smoke or vape.

Calum went out after half an hour of being there. As he was passing where John sat he took a cigar from his pocket and removed the cellophane from it, ready to light up as soon as he was outside.

John waited 5 minutes then walked out to join him.

Calum was standing on his own, leaning over a fence and looking out to the fields beyond.

'Good result,' John said by way of introduction.

'Gets harder every time. Not as young as I was. This will be my last,' Calum said, without looking to see who he was talking to.

'What kind of lad was Colin?'

Calum quickly turned.

'Colin. Oh, it's you copper. Why are you asking?'

'Well, you aren't stupid, so I won't bullshit you. I am looking into the cold case of his killing.'

'What, they put a uniformed sergeant on the case. Obviously not a priority to solve it.'

'I am a Detective Sergeant. I've only been on the case for a week, but I am already making inroads.'

The comment was a bit tongue in cheek, but he wanted Calum to open up. He hadn't much time, the cigar had been smoked down about a third.

'Colin was a quiet boy. Clever, good looking, had it all going for him. He wanted to be a schoolteacher. History if I remember right. His father was pushing him to play football full-time.'

'What about girls? Was he, you know, playing about with anybody he shouldn't have been?'

Calum looked away and blew out a plume of smoke before he answered.

'I know what you are thinking, was he poking it where he shouldn't. Maybe somebody took revenge. No, he wasn't that kind of lad.'

Calum turned and blew out a big puff of smoke and followed it with a little spit.

'Did he have any enemies?'

'No. He hadn't a bad bone in his body, everybody liked him.'

'Have you no idea who might have killed him?'

Calum turned and looked John square in the eyes.

'If I had any idea, now or then, would I not have said? Of course, I would.'

John continued looking in his eyes before Calum turned away and inhaled deeply on his cheroot.

'There was a rumour the taxi driver might have been a suspect, but he was never traced,' John put to him. He had read that in the case book.

'We said that at the time. How could you not trace the driver? After all he was Polish, well at least foreign and was a ringer for Tony Blair.'

'What if it wasn't him?'

Calum never answered, but just shook his head gently.

'I think you know more about this than you have ever let on. Something happened that night and you 3 know more than you have ever let on.'

Calum drew on his cigar again and threw it to the ground before stamping it out. As he walked away he glimpsed back. but never spoke.

'McDowall next,' John said to himself before heading back to the hall.

John sat back on his seat away from the hubbub from the tables the players, old and new, were seated.

A few minutes later Calum went over and spoke to Isaac McDowall. Out of the corner of his eye John could see the once tricky winger look over in his direction. The team captain undoubtedly marking his card about him.

A hush descended as the raffle began. Prize after prize given out but even with 20 strips of tickets John couldn't get even close to winning anything.

Raffle over, a microphone was readied in the middle of the small stage at the front of the hall.

The amateur team's official, the guy who invited John over to the purvey, walked over and stood behind the mike.

'Ladies and gents, big thanks for to you all for turning up today and supporting this event. Before we continue I think it's only right we start with a minute's silence in memory of Colin Fisher.'

The hall was hushed, except for the occasional cough and some small kids speaking and being quickly hushed by anxious parents.

After the minute the old guy spoke again.

'Thank you again. As you know this is all for charity and we asked Colin Fisher's parents who we should donate the monies raised to and they asked it be presented to the youth team as Colin loved his time playing with the team.'

This got a round of applause.

'Thanks. I can reveal the amount raised so far with almost all money counted, is £372 and this will be passed on to the youth team.'

This got a further round of applause.

'Well done to the Crocks team, I would now like to ask Calum Hunter up to the stage to say a few words.'

Calum got up from his seat and strode purposefully to the mike. He was applauded and raised his hands to acclaim it.

'Well, what can I say, the Crocks did it again.'

Their was applause and other cat calls, this time was from where the Crocks were sitting while there was friendly booing from the Amateurs area.

'Although Hoody did the business again.'

All eyes turned to where Davy Hood was sitting, and he raised a glass in salute.

'It was once again a team effort and shows that quality wins in the end. Unfortunately, the young team won't be able to get their revenge as we have decided this will be the last time the Crocks play together.'

There were sighs, and more gentle booing again while John looked to where the Crocks sat. They all looked bemused, shocked at the news, except for Isaac McDowall who looked downward.

'I think we are all getting too old for this, and I know I will be sore for 3 days after this. Once again, big thanks to everybody who have turned up at these events over the years and did a bit of good for charity in Colin's name. Thanks again.'

John was surprised that he only mentioned Colin's name right at the end, almost as if it was a forethought.

After this there was a scraping of chairs as people started leaving.

John kept his focus on the Crocks area but more so, as he watched Isaac. Most folk were there with families, but he seemed to be alone. He was the first of the Crocks to get up to leave.

Teammates all got up to shake his hand and it was obvious he was about to leave and wanted away as soon as possible.

John went out before him hurried to the car park to get his car then sat in it waiting for him. If Isaac's parents were still staying locally he might be paying them a visit before he left.

Fortunately for John Isaac's car was also parked in the car park. Isaac got into his car, a fancy BMW with a private plate which almost spelled Isaac. As he drove off John followed.

The car headed for the estate where his parents still stayed, according to Hamish. John followed and it drove through the estate and stopped at the lane down where Colin's dead body had been found.

Isaac got out of his car and went down the lane.

John parked further down the street and waited a few minutes before heading down the lane after Isaac. He found him standing silently in front of where the body had lain, head bowed.

When he turned to leave he saw John waiting at the top of the lane.

He walked toward him shaking his head gently. Before the cop could talk Isaac raise a hand and pointed a finger at him.

'I have nothing to say to you.'

'Why? Don't you want justice done? Your mate died down there and his parents haven't had justice.'

'Have you spoke to them? They have moved on. They don't expect your lot will ever find out who killed Colin. When you do this you just rake things up and give them more hurt.'

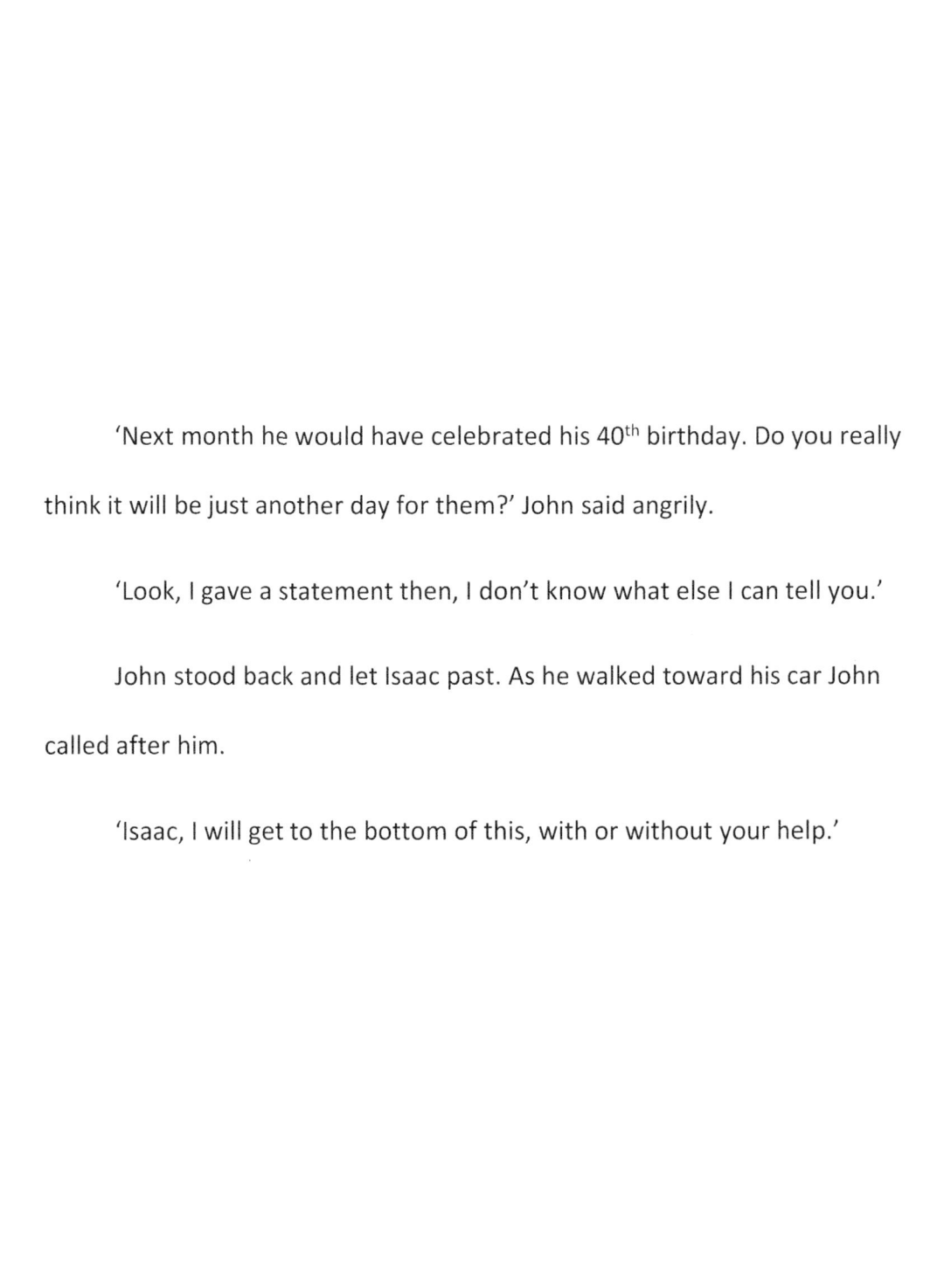

'Next month he would have celebrated his 40th birthday. Do you really think it will be just another day for them?' John said angrily.

'Look, I gave a statement then, I don't know what else I can tell you.'

John stood back and let Isaac past. As he walked toward his car John called after him.

'Isaac, I will get to the bottom of this, with or without your help.'

SIX

Next morning John wrote up his notes, with every little bit he could remember. Often it was small pieces of info, snippets, that gave clues to help solve cases like this.

When he finished this he searched through the dust topped boxes of old records from the previous investigations and found the statements for Calum Hunter, Isaac McDowall and Davy Hood. They were all dated 7th June, 4 days after Colin's body was found.

Calum's was first and contained little detail. They went to the dancing, headed for the Coffee boat, a coffee bar where people hung about after the dancing to get a coffee to sober up but more importantly to have a last chance at pulling a bird, as he said. Then they got in a taxi and headed home. The taxi driver was Polish and looked like Tony Blair.

They got out the taxi at the end of Hunter Avenue and they went their separate ways.

Isaac's was practically word for word. John shook his head, surely Davy's was different. When he skim read it he saw it was almost identical. It was also practically word for word. Sure they had all experienced the same thing that night but John smelled a rat.

In the 4 days since Colin's dead body was found the 3 had 4 days to corroborate their stories. Obviously that was what they did. Why, John asked himself.

One thing that got John angry was sloppy detective work. Firstly, he would have had them in the Police Station the next day, no later. Then he would have badgered the 3 for more details. What about the other things that could be important, was there any incident at the dancing or at the Coffee boat afterwards? What about the taxi driver, was there anything said to him that might have offended him?

The report was written by D.C. Andrew Coats. John remembered him when he started in uniform and spent a few months in Kilmarnock as part of his training. Coats was in his early 60's and counting the days until he retired. That was no excuse for shoddy work, John thought.

What he needed to do was lean on the 3 guys, they knew more than they were saying. He would start with Davy Hood that afternoon.

John was about to knock on the door on the Hood's bungalow when it suddenly opened. A shocked white-haired woman was surprised to see somebody standing there. She had a bottle of water in her hand and was obviously heading out with it.

'Sorry to bother you, you must be Mrs. Hood.'

'Yes,' she said, wondering who the neatly suited man was. She wasn't expecting anybody.

'I am Detective Sergeant John Rose. I work cold cases and I am currently working on the murder of Colin Fisher.'

'Oh right.'

'I was looking to speak to Davy. Is he in?'

He maybe should have asked if he was fit to talk, it was after 1 in the afternoon, he would probably sleeping be off his latest bag of booze.

'He is out the back in the man cave.'

'Oh, right. Is he sleeping it off.'

'No,' his mother interrupted, and with a face that showed she wasn't happy with his suggestion.

'He is still on one of his fitness drives. Hasn't had a drink since Friday. He goes all out on his fitness for a while then he will relapse and take a drink and go back on the drink full-time. Here, take this water down to him.'

John took the bottle that was already wet with condensation. He made his way down the side of the house and saw a beautifully constructed garden room at the back of the garden as Mrs.Hood had said. A definite man cave.

He knocked on the door and waited before walking in.

'You don't need to knock!' he must have shouted but the room so well constructed the sound was severely muffled.

John walked in and saw him working with dumbbells.

Davy didn't even look round but concentrated on his routine.

'Forty-nine, fifty,' he said then sat them down. Turning, he looked surprised to see the policeman standing there with his water.

'Oh, it's you. Thought I had seen the last of you yesterday.'

'Like a bad penny, I always seem to turn up when least expected or probably wanted.'

'I've got nothing to say.'

'Just give me 5 minutes. Then if you still don't want to talk I will walk away.'

Davy took the water off him and sat on the bench press and signalled for him to start.

'Right, first off, we didn't get off on the right foot last week. I was out of order ambushing you like I did. Secondly, I didn't ask to be put on a job like this, you know, working cold cases that other folk before me couldn't solve. Now I have the case I will do all I can to solve, even if I ruffle a few feathers on the way.

I have read transcripts of your interviews. Almost word for word.

The way I see it, the 3 of you that were with that night with Colin all agreed to keep your stories the same. For whatever reason I don't know yet but what I have seen that since then the other 2 have gotten on with their lives, good jobs, family, fancy cars whereas you have born the burden, been hung out to dry by them.'

Davy listened but still wasn't willing to say anything.

'After yesterday's announcement by Calum it would seem they aren't even willing to come back to the village. The memory of that night too much for them but you stay here.

I bet you think about Colin and what happened every day.'

Davy looked to the floor now.

'Am I right?'

Davy looked up and now had tears in his eyes.

'Tell me everything, it will be cathartic, getting it all off your chest.'

Davy put the bottle down and wiped his eyes with the bottom of his vest top.

'What do you want to know?'

'Everything that happened that night, from the beginning.'

'Right. We played football that afternoon and met up at 7 o'clock in the tap shop. That's what we called the pub next to the Spar shop down the village. We had a beer there then went round the corner and got the bus to Ayr. We had a beer in 1 of the pubs in Ayr then headed for the dancing in the Club De Mar.

After the dancing we followed a group of birds down to the Coffee Boat, you know, chasing our hole. There were 4 birds and they all seemed up for it.'

Davy looked round to the policeman.

'You know what I mean by that?'

'Of course, do you think I didn't go chasing after sex when I was that age?'

'Anyway, they were having none of it, so we went looking for a taxi. There was a guy waiting in the next street in a licensed cab. We made a joke because the license plate was No.69.'

'Hold on, do you mean the car registration, or the taxi license plate had a 69 on it?'

'Do you mean his taxi plate or his number plate?'

'The number plate. Don't remember any of the rest of it, you know the letters but the numbers were 69. We tried joking with the guy about it, but he was a johnny foreigner.'

'What do you mean?'

'Polish I think, called us boss all the time. He was a ringer for Tony Blair, you know the Prime Minister at that time. He wasn't daft though. We asked how much to Crosshouse. He asked us how far it was, and I think Hunter said it was 10 miles. He said it was £15.

We drove away and just before Dundonald he stopped the car in a lay-by and said that was 10 miles. He was smart enough to set his mileometer and not believe 4 drunk guys. So, we agreed to give him another fiver and he drove on. We all got out at Hunter Street and went our own way.'

'Who paid the driver?' John asked.

For somebody who had suddenly shown almost total recall to a night 22 years previously, Davy suddenly stalled. He looked down at his hands and swallowed hard before answering.

'Colin was in the front, he paid him.'

He was lying John was sure but believed everything else he had told him was true. Suddenly, in his eyes, this foreign taxi driver had suddenly become a suspect. In fact, it looked like he might be the only suspect he could get.

'Why did you not give the detectives this level of information at the time?'

'They never asked. Plus, Calum told us to keep shtum.'

'Calum did. Why?'

'To tell you the truth, he didn't like Colin much. He was too full of himself, bragging about what he had, and it was his fault we struck out with the girls at the Coffee Boat.'

'How, what did he do?'

'There were 4 girls and we planned to nab 1 each. He said something to the Calum who had a go at him. After that the girls got in their taxi and blew us out.'

'What did he say?'

'I never found out. Calum said we would chin him the next day. When I asked Calum what he meant he said by chin him he meant ask him, not hit him.'

'What about Calum then? Could he have done it?'

'Done what? Oh, you mean kill Colin? I suppose he could have but no way did he.'

'Well, he did ask you to keep quiet?'

John let that one hang in the air. Davy let it hang there and didn't answer it.

'So, what now, do I need to give a statement?'

'Not just now, but I hope this has given you some kind of closure. Stay off the booze and start your life again.'

Davy nodded.

'Right, I need to go back through the files from back at the time and see if they spoke to the taxi driver.'

John excused himself and let himself out leaving Davy to pick up the dumbbells again.

SEVEN

John found the files on the interviews with the taxi drivers in Ayr. The main "suspect", the driver of the cab with the 69 on his number plate.

That year, 2000, there were only 27 registered taxis in South Ayrshire that year and all 27 were interviewed.

The driver of the now infamous car with the numbers 69 on it turned out to be called Ernie McLean. The car licensed to the plate was a 1997 Peugeot 306 according to the statement.

Mr. McLean was at his caravan near Dumfries that whole weekend and he was ruled out. His car was on the driveway all weekend. According to the record the caravan park was contacted, and they agreed he was there.

John noted there was no mention of anybody corroborating the car being sat on the drive the whole time he was away. Too late to do that now.

John wrote on his notebook to ask Davy and the other 2 what kind of car they were driven home in. If they remembered.

The other 26 taxi drivers all had alibis, and none were reported as Polish or looking like the Tony Blair, the Prime Minister at that time. After that the taxi driver route wasn't pursued any further.

John's next step was to find out about this Ernie McLean and the Polish Tony Blair look-alike. Most conventional detectives would have been on the phone to taxi licensing at South Ayrshire. John, being far from orthodox in his methods, headed to the main taxi rank in Ayr town centre to speak to any drivers he found waiting on the rank.

First though, he was making a detour via Crosshouse to speak to Davy Hood.

John Rose parked his car in the Matalan car park, just round from the taxi rank. It was just after 1 o'clock, and he expected most cabbies would be trying to grab a bite to eat.

There were 3 cars parked up. The front driver was sitting in his car, hoping for a quick hire now after waiting his turn for who knows how long.

John walked round to driver's door, he didn't want him to get excited about a hire or make him lose his turn.

When he opened his window he could see the guy would have only been 30 at the most.

'Sorry to bother you.' John flashed his i.d. badge. 'I am trying to trace an Ernie McLean who was a cabby 20 years ago.'

The guy simply shook his head. 'Sorry mate, never heard of him.'

John thanked him and headed to the next cab. It was empty, the 2 drivers standing at the wall next to the rank, drinking coffee.

'Hi guys. D.S. John Rose, I am trying to trace an Ernie McLean who was a cabbie 20 years ago.'

The 2 drivers looked at each other then they shook their heads.

One guy, all bushy red beard and hair looked at John as he stroked his beard.

'Twenty years ago? You will be lucky mate.'

'How long have you 2 been cabbying?'

'I've been doing it for 8 years and Charlie, what are you, 6 years?' beardy said.

'No, nearly 7 and a ½.'

'Really mate. Time flies. I don't know anybody who has been around that long.'

'What about old Albert?' Charlie asked Beardy.

'Oh, Christ your right. Albert Blakely I think he is called. Drives an old black cab.'

'Of course, he just works part time now,' Charlie said.

'So, do you think he will be working today?' the policeman asked.

'Who knows? Just does it to get away from the wife I think. Must be terrible to be retired, spending 24/7 with the trouble and strife,' beardy said.

John shook his head gently; it certainly was a thought, spending all day with the wife.

'Think I will get a cuppa while I'm waiting. Where do you recommend?'

'The places round the front here are all poncy and that means expensive. Nip down round to the left there, café down there is more homely and cheaper,' Charlie advised, with a wink.

'Thanks lads.'

John headed back with his cuppa and roll in sausage, most of which he had scoffed on the way back to the rank. When the rank was in view he could see the taxis that had been there were gone and there was a black cab sitting second now. Chances were it was Albert. John dropped his roll in the first bin he came to and headed for the cab as quick as he could, trying not to spill his hot tea as he went.

Albert was sitting comfortable in his cab with a cup of something from his flask in its plastic cup.

'Albert, is it?' John asked between gasps.

'Sure son.'

John smiled, he hadn't been called son for years and hadn't expected to be called it at 62 years of age.

'I am looking for information about Ernie McLean, he was a cabbie about 20 years ago.'

'That's right. Nice guy was Ernie.'

'Was?'

'Yeah, died oh,' Albert looked to the roof of the cab as he trawled his memory. 'About 8 years ago. Quite sudden but he had retired by then. Good darts player he was. They said he could have gone pro but there was no money in it then. Not like now.'

'What about a Polish driver about that time?'

'Yeah. Ernie sold his car and licence to John or Jan, something like that he was called. He was his son-in-law. He was foreign right enough, might have been Lithuanian or Polish.'

'He didn't drive at the same time as Ernie, did he? You know, share the driving?'

'What, before he bought it? Could have done, I am not sure. He is still driving a cab. Drives a flash white Mercedes now.'

'Does he do the rank?'

'Yeah, but he doesn't work during the day as far as I remember, does nights. More money nights if you do the hours.'

'Thanks Albert.'

John rested against the wall at the rank and drank his tea before heading back to get his car.

'I love it when a plan comes together,' he said to himself as he went.

EIGHT

John drove home that afternoon feeling on top of the World. He felt all the pieces were falling into place, like a jigsaw.

After he left the taxi rank he called into the main Police Station in Ayr and spoke to the C.I.D. there. Turned out they had never had any reports about a Polish taxi driver called Jan or John having ever been in any bother or even knew who he was.

He also organised for 2 beat bobbies to accompany him that evening as he went looking for this Polish John or Jan. If he worked nights they would hopefully catch up with him or surely find another late-night driver who knew him and maybe where he lived.

The smile on his face didn't last long when his phone rang, and the hands-free display flashed up that it was D.I. Walker was calling.

'Afternoon sir.'

'Yes, quite. How's the investigation going, John?'

'Very well, as it happens. The lads were taken home in a taxi driven by a Polish or other foreign national who looked like Tony Blair. I am hoping to catch up with him tonight.'

'Nice of you to let me know.' The D.I. said with a bitter barb to his voice.

'It just happened this afternoon and I am on my way back to the station.'

'The thing is, I have just had Ayr C.I.D. on the blower and they are not happy you haven't gone through proper channels.'

John seethed. That was one of the things that was wrong with modern day Policing, too much paperwork and hoops to jump through to get things done.

'The thing is, I was in Ayr anyway and it was easier to drop into the station there.'

'I am on the end of a phone. Your superior should speak to their superior. Proper channels John.'

'Okay sir, I will know in the future.'

'Right, I want your up-to-date report by the end of play today.'

'Yes, sir,' John said, while giving a single digit salute to the screen.

That buggered up John's plans. He had wanted to get home and have his dinner and spend a bit of time with his wife because he felt if he did run into this Polish guy it could be a long night for him.

Before he left the Saltcoats Station that night he knocked on his boss's door.

'I have emailed you the report on the case so far. As you will probably know I have arranged for 2 uniformed officers to accompany me tonight. I assume it will be okay for me to claim any extra hours as overtime.'

'Assume, John makes an ass of u and me.' Walker said in his smarmiest of voices.

'I take it you do want this case solved.'

'Yes, but modern Policing techniques would simply be that you find out where this Polish man lives and go to his abode and talk to him there.'

'Yes, of course, sir. However, I prefer to meet folk where they least expect it, that's where their guard is likely to be down. Suddenly they feel vulnerable, not in a safe space and they are likely to say the wrong thing. That is as far as they are concerned, not us.'

'How much overtime are you expecting then?'

'With a bit of luck, I could end up nightshift tonight and have this guy wrapped up quickly. If that is the case I take tomorrow off, and it would only be a few hours.'

'I think we could stretch to that. If that is the case I hope you would leave an update before you clock off for the night.'

'Yes, of course, sir,' John said through gritted teeth. He would need to come all the way back to Saltcoats then double back to Irvine again at the end of his shift. A lot of extra miles and time just to keep Walker happy.

John parked the car in the secure parking at Ayr Police station just before 8 that night. The officers arranged to accompany him were already in their marked car waiting on him and he slipped in the back.

He introduced himself and found out his companions were P.C.'s Warnock and Booth. They were both around 30 years old and looked as if they could handle themselves.

Neither knew who the Polish taxi driver was but had seen the white Mercedes cab on the streets.

At the rank John got out and told the other 2 to hang loose. What he meant was they weren't confined to the car, but he needed them to be around when or if needed.

There were 5 taxis sitting on the rank when he arrived. No white Merc but an array of different vehicles. As he was crossing the road the 1st cab drove away and the rest moved forward 1 space.

John headed to the front car before he disappeared. The driver was a woman who looked pretty with long blond hair until she turned to face him when he knocked on the passenger window.

Looking round he could tell she was as old as him if not older. Her skin was tanned and wrinkled, very wrinkled, and she had thick black drawn on eyebrows.

Before she could speak John flashed his i.d.

The electric window slid down when she hit the button.

'Hi. I am looking for John or Jan, the Polish taxi driver. Do you know him, he drives a white Mercedes?'

'Sorry love, this is my first week on the rank.'

'Okay, thanks anyway.'

Next in the rank was a sort of cross between a car and a van. The driver saw him talk to the woman in front and slid his passenger window down before John reached him.

'Hello sir, D.S. John Rose. I am looking for the Polish driver, car is a white Merc.'

'Right, you mean Jan. He was here earlier, left about 20 minutes ago. He will probably be due back anytime.'

'Cheers mate.'

John walked over to the marked Police car and told them their target was due back anytime. He also told them he planned to ask him to go to Ayr Police station with him. If he refused he would signal them, and they would take him into custody.

Just at that John saw a white Mercedes with a taxi sign on the roof heading up the hill on his left, heading for the back of the rank.

'Showtime,' he said to his force colleagues before crossing the road to greet the white car's driver.

The driver joined the rank and reached for a bottle of water.

John knocked on his door and showed his i.d.

The driver gave him the thumbs up, and John opened the passenger door and slid in beside him.

Jan was a big guy, quite muscular, either he had been a labourer in the past or worked out. He had black hair that was now flecking with bits of grey and when he turned to look at John it was evident he had been attractive as a younger man. The lads had been right, even now there was a look of Tony Blair about him. This was definitely the man he was after.

'Hello sir, I am Detective Sergeant John Rose. You are the brother-in-law of Ernie McLean, is that right?'

'No boss, was. He was my brother-in-law, but he died.'

John was angry with himself for the slip, he knew fine well Ernie was dead, but he was also glad because he had his man.

'You bought his car and licence off him.'

'Yes boss.'

'What is your name?'

'Jan Banka.'

'Well Jan, what I want to know about was before then. You used to drive his cab at the weekends when he was at the caravan, is that correct?'

The Polish man took another swig of water from his bottle as he considered his answer.

'Yes, boss, on Friday and Saturday nights. Ernie didn't know.'

'I think we need to continue this interview at the Police station. Do you agree to come with me?'

The big man thought for a little longer than John wanted.

'There is a Police car there. If you don't want to go with me you can go in the car with them.'

The worry on the man's face grew.

'But boss, my girl she was pregnant. Babies cost a lot of money.'

'Okay, best you don't say anything more at the moment. Now are we going to the Police station or are you going with me or them?'

'Let's go,' he said and started his engine up.

As they drove away the cars at the front of the rank blasted their horns, thinking Jan had jumped the queue and stolen their fare but stopped when they saw the cop car following him.

NINE

John Rose led Jan Banko into the interview room. They were joined by D.C. Jack Simpson, the duty detective that evening.

The D.C. started the tape for the interview and identified those in the room before John started asking the questions.

'Jan, I asked you before but for the tape do you wish to have a lawyer present?'

Jan shook his head.

'For the tape you need to speak. Everything you say needs to be clear for the tape.'

'No. No solicitor. I have done nothing wrong.'

'Right, you are Jan Banko and you are a registered taxi driver.'

'Correct.'

'How did you become a taxi driver?'

'My brother-in-law owned a taxi before me and when he gave it up he sold it to me.'

'Who was your brother-in-law?'

'Ernie McLean. I married his younger sister Helen.'

'When did you take ownership of the taxi?'

The big man put his hands in his head as he thought about it. He counted out silently on his fingers.

'2007.'

'When did you get your licence as a driver?'

'2001.'

'Who did you drive for between 2001 and 2007?'

'I worked full-time as a labourer on building site but do some shifts for Ernie or his friends at the weekends.'

'Did you ever drive any taxis before you got your licence.'

'You know this, I told you earlier.'

'For the tape Jan. We need it on record.'

'Yes. Before this when Ernie went to his caravan at the weekend, and we were staying with him at the time I some nights took the taxi out.'

Suddenly his eyes lit up, as if some frightening thought came to him.

'I won't lose my licence because of this?' he said, as he looked from one inquisitor to the other.

'No, we aren't here to do that. What I need to know is what happened one particular night when you were out in the cab. On the night between June the third and June the fourth in 2000, you took a group of 4 lads from the Coffee Boat to Crosshouse.'

'2000? That was 22 years ago. How do I remember?'

'Well, they remember you.'

Jan looked down at his hands as he tried to recollect.

'You were doing it illegally so you must have been watching what you were doing?'

'Yes, now I think I remember. I parked away from the busy. The boys ask me how much to Crosshouse. I say how far, and they say only 10 miles. £15 I say and they get in. I set milometer and when we get to the 10 miles I stop in layby and say 10 miles, where do you want off. They laugh as if joke but joke on them, I was not stupid Polish man. So, they say few miles more and will pay £20.'

'Do you remember anything about the lads? Was there fighting or anything?'

'No. Madonna came on radio and boy in front kept singing the song even after it finished. Boy in back kept tell him shut up. Got really angry boss. I said I would stop and throw him out and they both shut up.'

'So, what happened when you got to Crosshouse?'

'Guy in front said he had money and needed to get out to get money from pocket. The boys got out and started to walk away. I put down window and boy walked slowly round to my window then he shouted run and they all ran away.'

'What did you do?'

'I got out and chased him with my persuader.'

'Persuader?'

'Ernie had a baseball bat and he kept it beside his seat. It was only to warn people, you know.'

'So, what happened next?'

'Boy from front ran down street and down lane. I caught up and hit him on the leg. He fell and just lay there. I got his wallet out of his back pocket and took the £20 out then threw it on the ground. I am not thief, just took what I am owed.'

John nodded then threw in the verbal grenade.

'That boy, Colin Fisher, was found on the spot where you left him later that morning. He was dead, his head had been bashed in.'

There was a look of terror on Jan Banko's face.

'No boss, not me. I didn't bash him in, I didn't kill him. I just hit his leg, not his head. He might have hit his head when he fell, but he was not bashed in when I left him. No way boss.'

John looked to his fellow detective but said nothing.

'Honest boss, I just hit his leg, not bash his brains out. No way.'

'I never said you did, Jan. I am just getting the facts from that night. You are saying when you left him he was alive but unconscious.'

'Yes boss.'

Jan put his hands over his face.

'Okay, Jan, we will need you to stay for a while longer. Do you agree to give a DNA sample and have your fingerprints taken?'

Jan took his hands down and looked stunned by what he had just heard and the position he was now in.

'It's to eliminate you, Jan. We are not trying to blame you.'

Jan nodded. 'Okay boss,' but didn't look as if he believed him.

'As I said, you will need to stay for a while, until we check some things out.'

'But my wife, she will be expecting me.'

'It's okay, you are allowed to call her.'

John opened the interview room door and the uniform who was standing outside escorted Jan through to the holding area of the custody suite.

With the tape off John turned to the other detective.

'I know a bit of the background to this, but you are coming into this fresh. What's your feelings?'

'Seems like he is telling the truth. Or he is a great actor.'

'Yes, I am thinking along those lines, but I am still not convinced. He has had over 20 years to get his story straight in his head. If he had been duped like that before, losing the cab fare, then maybe he took his wrath out on the poor lad that night?'

'Tell you what we do, we let him sleep on it. We can keep him until, what, 9 o'clock tomorrow night. Maybe he will remember something else by then.'

'Right, sir. You are in charge of the case.'

By the time John drove to the Saltcoats station, wrote out his report, emailed it to Walker, then travelled home to Irvine it was after 1 a.m. in the morning before he got back home.

He felt drained, both mentally and physically shattered. He couldn't wait to get into bed.

After he got out of the bathroom and opened the bedroom door slightly Karen called out to him.

'I've been waiting up for you. Go and shower.'

A smile cracked on his face. Maybe he wasn't so tired after all.

John woke and realised after a few seconds he was in bed alone. The alarm clock informed him it was 10:13. Somehow, although he went out like a light after their lovemaking, he still felt tired. He couldn't lie on though; he would be expected back at the cop shop by 12.

Karen had tea and toast on the table by the time he got down the stairs.

'You were restless last night. Usually after, you know, you are sound. Apart from the snoring.'

John never spoke about cases with Karen, but he realised this latest one was going round in his head, and he needed to speak to some-one about it.

'Right, remember I said about the taxi, and you said they did a runner, well you were right.'

Karen smiled but didn't go as far as saying I told you so, which she usually would.

'The thing that bothers me is the other 3 lads that were in the taxi have kept quiet about that night for 22 years. Not helping us with our enquiries. What does that say to you?'

Karen drank from her teacup as she thought.

'They must be involved,' she said. 'Must be, why else would they not want justice for the boy? After all he was their mate, wasn't he.'

'Yes, they all played football together. You know that's what's been going round in my head. They are either involved or know more about it. They must do. I need to speak to the other 2 lads.'

TEN

John walked into Saltcoats Police station just before 12 o'clock that day. He planned to head over to Crosshouse to speak to Isaac McDowall's parents and get their son's phone number to arrange a meeting with him.

Cathy, the woman on the front desk welcomed him with a smile.

'Detective Inspector Walker wants to see you, said to grab you as you walk in the door you have to go to his office.'

'I was hoping you would grab me first,' he said, flirting before he left.

'What does he want me for, did he say?' he added.

'He just said congratulations were in order.'

'Oh no,' John said, shaking his head. Then he wondered if there had been developments in the Fisher case while he had been in bed.

John knocked gently on his boss's office door.

When Walker looked up and saw him a broad, cheesy grin swept over his face, and he ushered him in with hasty hand gestures.

'Well done Sergeant.'

'Why, what's happened?'

'What? You arrested the taxi driver.'

'No, he is only in custody. Has something happened since I left Ayr? Has he confessed?'

'No, but he confessed to hitting Colin Fisher.'

'Hitting, yes. Not killing him. I don't think he did it?'

'He must have. I was going to arrange a Press conference.'

'That's premature. I want to speak to the other 2 guys that were in the taxi with Fisher that night first. McDowall and Hunter.'

Walker's mood turned dark instantly.

'I have been singing your praises all morning. John Rose has solved this murder case in double quick time, that's what I've been saying. Now you say you have jack shit. This makes me look stupid.'

John, for once, didn't say the first thing that came into his mind, he would have been disciplined if he did.

'Look, I think I am pretty close to getting to the bottom of this. Bear with me.'

'Well, you better go then. Remember, the clock's ticking.'

John went straight to his office and set about looking for the McDowall's address. Must be somewhere he thought but gave up after 10 minutes. There were so many boxes of evidence it would have been like looking for a needle in a haystack, he conceded. He hadn't written it in his notes either, that wasn't like him.

Plan B, he knew where the Hoods lived, surely either Davy or his mother could furnish him with the McDowall's address.

Mrs. Hood seemed genuinely pleased to see John when he knocked on her door.

'My, I don't know what you said to our Davy, but he has been so different since your little chat the other day. Is it him you are looking for?'

'No, it's actually the McDowall's address I am looking for, you know, Isaac's parents.'

'Now I don't know the address but if you go back and go into the 2nd cul-de-sac and, let me think, well I don't know the number but it's the house with the big tree out front. You can't miss it.'

'Right, thanks. I am glad Davy's doing better, he seems a nice lad.'

She was right, he couldn't miss it. The tree in the front garden was huge and dominated the whole front garden.

John knocked on the door. Inside he heard a woman's voice telling another person to answer the door.

There was a pause, a turning of a key in the lock then the door swung open.

Mister McDowall was holding a copy of the Daily Express and looked at John over the top of a pair of half-moon spectacles. He was wearing a cardigan and shirt and cream chinos.

John held up his i.d. 'Sorry to bother you, sir, I wanted a word about Isaac.'

'Oh, there's nothing wrong is there?' he asked, suddenly with a bit of panic in his voice.

'No. Sorry I should have introduced myself. I am Detective Sergeant John Rose. I am from Scottish Police, and I am working cold cases. Currently I am working on the murder of Colin Fisher, and I am looking to speak to Isaac.'

'Oh, he doesn't live here.'

'Yes I know, but I don't have current contact details for him.'

'Listen, you better come in.'

They walked through to the lounge.

'Take a seat.'

The 3-piece suite seemed too large for the room and left little room for anything else. John sat in one of the chairs while his host folded his paper and sat it on the coffee table that was in front of the sofa.

'So, is it Isaac's address or just his phone number you need?'

'Both would be ideal.'

'Jane, where is Isaac's address?'

'What?' he heard call out from somewhere else in the bungalow.

She beringed through and seemed ready to have words with her hubby when she saw they had a visitor and her mood changed instantly.

'Oh, hello.'

'John is a policeman; he is looking into Colin Fisher's death. He wants Isaac's address and phone number.'

'It's in the phone book,' she said, exasperated at her husband's ineptitude.

She disappeared into the hall.

'Oh, I am Andy and as you know my wife is Jane. Would you like a coffee? Or maybe something stronger.'

'Tea would be fine.'

Jane appeared and John got his notebook out.

While she read out the information John asked for her husband nipped through to the kitchen and put the kettle on, which was just off the living room.

Andy re-joined him while Jane swapped places with and tended to the teacups.

'The murder of Colin Fisher must have had an effect on Isaac,' John said as way of an icebreaker.

'It affected us all. Back then we rarely locked our doors, except at night of course. We still keep them locked, even during the day. It was just a habit we got into back then, but, well, there is still a killer out there. They never caught them.'

'Sure, that's why I am here. Of course, I can't say too much about an active case, even when it is over 20 years old, but I feel I am making progress.'

'Why has it taken until now though?'

'I can't speak for other investigations but when I get a case I get involved personally. I was at the charity football game on Sunday, meeting the locals and letting them know we haven't forgotten the terrible thing you have been living with all these years.'

'So, why do you need to speak to Isaac?'

'He was with Colin that night.'

'Surely he has given statements before. What more can he tell you?'

'It might surprise you but even the smallest piece of information could lead an investigation forward. I have spoken to Davy Hood, and he was very helpful.'

'Was he sober?' Andy asked.

He then went quiet when his wife arrived with a tray with the teacups with sugar and milk and a tray of chocolate biscuits.

As she did so the mention of Davy's name saw her exchanging looks with her husband.

'Do you learn from American detective shows on television?' Jane asked.

'No, I never watch them. My wife does and think we work like that in Scotland. You know she will ask if I subpoenaed anybody that day. Unfortunately, too much of our work nowadays involves paperwork.'

'It's the way of the world now,' Andy said, nodding in agreement.

'Does Isaac ever mention Colin or that night?'

Andy didn't seem forthcoming, so Jane spoke.

'No, he has kept it all to himself.'

'What does he do, you know for a job?'

Andy was suddenly keen to speak. 'He is a risk manager for a large insurance firm. He's based in Glasgow and has his own office.'

He was beaming now as he spoke proudly of his son's perceived achievement.

John could drink his tea hot, just out of the kettle hot and quickly drained his cup.

'Would you like another cup,' Jane asked.

'No, I need to get on. Thanks for everything,' he said and made his way out.

At the door Andy put out a hand to shake.

'Well, good luck with the investigation. Hope you get the eh. guilty one. It was nice to meet you.'

'Nice to meet you and your wife too Andy. Thank her for the tea.'

As John walked away he thought they were a nice couple, he just hoped it wasn't their son he was arresting.

John dialled Isaac's mobile number from the car while just outside his parent's house. It was answered after 3 rings.

'Hello, Isaac McDowall.'

'Hello sir. It's Detective John Rose from Police Scotland. I spoke to you briefly on Sunday. Now I need to speak to you officially. I am based in Saltcoats Police station and would prefer it if you could come here to be interviewed.'

'When are you talking about?'

'As soon as possible. Today preferably.'

'Today? I am at work in Glasgow today, wouldn't really be convenient.'

'It could be this evening if you like.'

'That's still not convenient.'

'Look sir, I am giving you the chance to come into the station of your own volition. The alternative is I send a car round either to your house or your workplace in Glasgow.'

John was playing it heavy, but he wanted to push the investigation along. He didn't like sitting twiddling his thumbs.

There was a silence as this threat sank in.

'I could be in Saltcoats for about 8 o'clock tonight,' he finally conceded.

'Fine. Ask for me, D.S.Rose, and I will see you then.'

ELEVEN

Isaac McDowall looked confident when he walked into the police station in Saltcoats. The P.C. who answered the bell request on the front desk called through to CID for D.S. John Rose who was through quite quickly.

'Hello. Isaac?'

'D.S. Rose,' Isaac said, offering a hand.

John shook it. His hand felt clammy to his touch.

'Thanks for coming in, this way please.'

He led him through to the CID and took him through and showed him into an interview room.

'Take a seat,' he said, 'just need a colleague to join us.'

'What is this an official interview?'

'Just procedure, sir,' John said, smiling as he said it.

'Am I a suspect?'

'Are you?' John said, then turned and left.

John walked through to the main office. Detective Constable Murray Long stood up when he saw him. John had already primed him about McDowall's interview.

John raised a hand to him.

'Take your time, Murray. That guy has probably never been interviewed by the Police as a possible suspect. At least that's what he seems to think.

If he sits in there for a few minutes it will play on his mind. Might even loosen his bowels.'

The D.C. laughed at his joke and added 'Good thinking, sir.'

'Mind games. Get in their heads.'

'How long do we wait?' Murray asked, keen to learn for the master.

'Well, he seemed cocky when I opened the door to let him through here but when I opened the interview room door and showed him in his face dropped. I think Isaac thought we were having a tea and biscuits meeting. Come on, that's enough, let's go.'

John let Murray go in front of him so that he could work the recording machine then he sat next to him.

'Before we start, do you want a lawyer present?' John asked.

'A lawyer? Why? I am not just here for an interview.' Isaac paused then added 'am I really suspect here?'

'Isaac, this may be a cold case, but it is still a murder inquiry, it needs to be recorded. You were possibly one of the last 4 people to see Colin, does that not make you at least under suspicion?'

'Well, I don't need a lawyer, my conscience is clear. I did nothing wrong that night.'

'Murray.'

The D.C. started the recorder then introduced the attendee's and repeated the question, asking Isaac if he required a lawyer which he again refused. Then he looked to John to start the questioning.

'Right, I spoke to Davy Hood the other day his version of what happened on the night of June the 3rd 2000. I would like your version of what happened that night.'

'I've given a statement before.'

'Yes. I've read it. I could have given that version of events and I wasn't even there that night. As I said, I have spoken to Davy Hood, and he gave me a full version of events that night. Very different from his statement.'

'You listened to an alcoholic and believed him?'

'Davy is off the sauce and is still angry that you and Calum decided the charity game was being cancelled.'

Isaac blew before continuing.

'We were having a good night in Ayr and ended up in Club de Mar. There was a group of 4 girls, we were trying to get off with them. Colin's folks were away for the weekend. and we were trying to get them to come back with us.

Anyway, we followed them to the Coffee boat. We were planning to get 2 taxis when something kicked off and the girls got in their taxi that had been booked. So, we got a taxi and headed home.

Back in Crosshouse we got let off in Hunter Street. Calum and I headed out onto the main street and the others went the other way.'

Isaac looked at the 2 detectives then shrugged and said, 'that's about it.'

'Right, here's where I am with that. You are a risk manager, correct.'

Isaac looked surprised.

'How do you,' was all he got out before John jumped in.

'I spoke to your parents today. Nice couple. Anyway, risk manager. You see I think I can put some of your thinking into my job.'

'What do you mean?'

'Well around 99% of murders are carried out by people who knew the victim. Of all the people who knew Colin, how many he knew would be in Hunter Street at that time in the morning. If you put those facts together, who would you say this points to?'

Isaac was quiet and looked down at the table. John kept quiet because they both knew the answer, but the detective wanted the other man to tell him.

'It points to the 3 of us and the taxi driver.'

Suddenly he looked up, as if it was the first time he had ever thought it could have been the cabbie.

'I think you are right. It certainly points to you 4. Now, I have spoken to Davy and the taxi driver, and I am happy to rule them out. That just leaves you 2.'

Isaac put his hands to his face.

They were disturbed by a knock on the interview room door.

A uniformed officer opened the door.

'Urgent call for you sir.'

The other detective paused the interview and John Rose stepped out of the room.

'Sir, it's a detective from Ayr. Times almost up with Jan Banko he said.'

'Right, I take it he hasn't said anything else. Tell him to release Banko without charge.'

'You don't want to speak to them?'

'No, I am busy here.'

The cop nodded and walked away.

John took a deep breath and re-entered the room. He gave a thumbs up to D.C. Long who restarted the recording.

'Right, Isaac. Time for the whole story. What really happened that night?'

Isaac took a deep breath.

'Right. The night had been going okay but as the night went on Colin started to brag about how rich his family were. How he could get anything he wanted. In fact, he could get anybody he wanted. I knew what he was like, but he was getting on Calum's wick.

We were at the Coffee boat and as I said we were chatting these girls up. Calum asked Colin what girl he fancied, and he said the blond girl because she looked like Calum's sister Erin.

Calum was raging and I had to calm him down. We were at the point when we were sorting out who was going in each taxi when Colin said to Calum that the new blond wouldn't be a virgin like Erin had been.

Calum's sister Erin was only 15 at the time. You can imagine how angry he was, and Calum made a grab for him. Davy and I had to hold him back. Then Colin said he was just winding him up but was laughing as he said it.

Just at that the girl's taxi that they had booked turned up and because of our fighting they got in it and left.'

'Fighting?' John asked.

'Well, not fighting but what would you call it? An altercation, maybe. That was it, with the girls away we decided to get a cab home. There was a taxi parked down the street from the Coffee boat and we got in it.

The driver was a Polish guy who looked like Tony Blair. We tried to get the taxi on the cheap because we knew as soon as the guy spoke he was foreign. Anyway, Colin was in the front, and we were in the back.

Calum had calmed a bit because I kept saying he was winding him up, told him it was just because Colin was drunk. Calum said when Erin watched the football team play she always said Colin was dishy.

The taxi driver had the radio on and the Madonna song, "Like a Virgin" came on and Colin started singing it, then turned round and looked straight at Calum then pointed to him. Calum tried to get forward to swing at him, but I held him back.

He couldn't get to him and said, if you have touched Erin I will kill you.'

'Do you think he meant it?' John asked.

'Right at that moment, yes. When we got to Crosshouse and the taxi parked up we got out. Colin had the taxi fare and we left him to pay. I guided Calum away from Colin and the car and up towards the main road which was down the lane at the end of the street.

We were walking away when Colin shouted run. We realised he wasn't going to pay the cabbie and was doing a runner. We hadn't planned it or anything. Anyway, Colin was the last one of us that needed to do that with all the money he had.

We just ran up to the main road. As we were walking home Calum was still raging at Colin and said he planned to go to his house and break one of his legs so he couldn't play for the team anymore.'

'Do you think he meant it?'

Isaac nodded. 'Yes.'

'So, why did you not tell all this back then?'

'Calum threatened me.'

'With what?'

Isaac put his head on his hands on the table. His shoulders moved up and down, when he raised his face there were tears in his eyes.

'Calum knew I was gay. Oh, growing up in a village like Crosshouse you wouldn't have survived if people knew you were gay. It's not like now where it's acceptable.'

'But you were chasing girls.'

'I suppose I was bisexual back then or just acting the straight guy to fit in. Since my wife divorced me 8 years ago I have been strictly gay, but I've not come out; my parents don't even know, it would kill them. They keep saying I should be looking for a new girl. It's probably why I rarely go and see them now.'

'Did Calum actually tell you he killed Colin?'

Isaac nodded then more tears welled in his eyes.

'He told me when he went home his young sister was still awake. He asked Erin if she had been out with Colin, and she said yes. When she told him they actually had sex he made up his mind to break his legs, both of them.

He got his baseball bat from the garage and set out for Colin's house. However, when he came across him unconscious in the lane at the park, he said he just lost it and gave him a thump on the head.

I was sworn to secrecy and Davy went along with him.'

'Why, what did he have on Davy?'

'Davy didn't know what happened that morning. He had started dabbling in drugs then, he was out his trumpet that night, he had taken E's.'

'Looks like you will need to come out to your parents now.'

'I had planned to wait until they were dead, but I will need to go tonight and tell them.'

'Oh, there was one other thing. On Sunday Calum said why don't we have a charity baseball game next year. He said he still had a bat, and he was laughing.'

'Right. Do you think he was telling you the truth?'

Isaac just nodded.

John then looked to the other policeman by his side who shook his head slightly, as if he knew what the senior officer was thinking.

'I'm sorry, Isaac, you will need to stay overnight after you give us your statement.'

'Why, I haven't done anything wrong?'

'Withholding information for over 20 years. Of course, you have now agreed to help us now. It will need to be put to the procurator fiscal in the morning who will decide what charges, if any, will be made.'

Isaac dried his eyes with the back of his hand.

'I'm sorry. I should have come forward before.'

'To tell you the truth, this should have come out in the investigation all those years ago.'

TWELVE

John Rose sat in his car at the Spar car park in Crosshouse, waiting on a phone call from Paisley Police to say Calum Hunter had been arrested and was on his way to Saltcoats nick. When he got the okay the plan was to raid Calum's parent's house on the long shot that the baseball bat, the murder weapon, was still there, and he had been telling Isaac the truth.

In a car next to him was a squad of 4 detectives from the local cop shop in Kilmarnock, waiting patiently as he did.

It had taken all day to get a search warrant signed by the local procurator. They finally got the paperwork at 4 o'clock and word was sent to Paisley to arrest Calum.

It was 10 minutes before 5 p.m. when John finally got the call to say Calum was in custody and was en-route to Saltcoats.

He started his engine and gave the other officers the thumbs up.

They headed round to the Hunter's bungalow, also in the Varney estate, 2 minutes away from the car park. John had driven past the house earlier and saw a car in the driveway and a light in the lounge, so he was sure there was somebody at home.

John rang the doorbell and knocked on the front door while he was joined by the other detectives.

Calum's mother looked astonished when she opened the door to John, who handed a copy of the search warrant which he handed her. She reached out absent-mindedly and took the paper from him.

'Police Scotland madam. This is a warrant to search your house and grounds for a possible weapon.'

'Weapon? What are you talking about? I think you have the wrong address. This is number 4.'

Just at that Calum's father appeared next to her.

'What the Hell is going on?'

'Mister Hunter, this is a warrant to search your premises for a weapon.'

'A weapon? What's this about?'

'The murder of Colin Fisher. Your son is currently in custody.'

'Colin's murder? You have Calum in custody, this is crazy.'

One of the detectives walked up to John.

'The garage is locked sir.'

'Have you got the garage keys, sir.'

Mrs.Hunter stepped back and lifted the keys off a hook and handed them to John, who passed them onto the other detective.

'The hut keys are on that too,' Calum's father called after him, 'but you are wasting your time.'

'Hold on,' he said and reached from behind the door for a jacket.

'Where are you going,' his wife said.

'I am going to watch them, make sure they aren't going to plant something. They do that, I have seen it on the telly.'

Mister Hunter then pushed past John and the other 2 detectives who went the opposite way into the house.

'Where do you want to look?' the frustrated housewife said.

'Is there any of Calum's stuff still in the house?'

'There might be some stuff in the loft.'

She pointed up to the square on the hall ceiling then handed John a handle for pulling the hatch down.

In the meantime, the other officers were looking through the other rooms.

John pulled the ladder down and made his way up. There was a cord and when he pulled it the loft area was bathed in bright light.

What he found was the usual junk and other jumble like Christmas trees, baubles and dusty suitcases. John put his disposable gloves on and started looking through the odds and ends.

It took him a short time to search it and came up empty.

When he stepped down the front door burst open, and a red-faced owner of the bungalow walked in.

'They've got a baseball bat and all my heavy tools, but it won't be the one you are looking for. This is a travesty.'

'Right, I will organise a receipt for it and anything else we take.'

John tried to sound matter of fact when he spoke, but his heart was racing. If this was the bat they were after Calum was bang to rights.

Outside the Kilmarnock detectives were waiting back at their car. They had the boot open, and the baseball bat was lying in the back still in the Tesco carrier bag they found it in. There was also a selection of other hammers and tools that would have done the job.

'Right, guys, thanks for your help. This could be mammoth in this case.'

When John arrived back to the Saltcoats station D.I. Walker was waiting for him. This was an occasion, although he hadn't been at the station long, he already had a reputation of being a strictly 9 to 5 cop. It was nearly 6 by then.

'John, how did it go?'

'We found a baseball bat. It was hidden in the eaves of the garage.'

'Brilliant, we've got him, then.'

'If there is Colin's DNA on it, yes.'

'He is in a cell and screaming for a lawyer.'

'What does that tell you? Guilty.'

'Yes. I thought I would sit in on the interview with you.'

'Sure, sir,' he said, but wished he could have anybody else in there.

When they finally made it to the interview room an hour later John was working the recording machine.

'Interview with Calum Hunter. Present are Calum Hunter, Detective Sergeant John Rose, Detective Inspector Kevin Walker and Mister Hunter's lawyer Sam Golder.

'Calum, going back to the night of June the 3rd into June the 4th, do you recall that night.'

'No comment.'

'I have a statement from Isaac McDowall that says you confessed to striking Colin Fisher on the head with a baseball bat. Is that true?'

'No comment.'

'We have a bat we found in your parent's garage. Is this the bat you used?'

'No comment.'

'If we find Colin's DNA on it how would you explain that?'

'No comment.'

D.I. Walker took the lead.

'Mister Hunter, how did you feel when Colin Fisher told you he had taken your sister's virginity?'

For a second the accused man's eyes gave away the cop had hit a nerve, but he calmed and again said, 'no comment.'

'Mister Golder, have you instructed your client to simply give no comment answers to all our questions?' D.I. Walker asked.

The lawyer looked at the detective.

'Mister Walker, my client is here under false pretences and with what little so-called proof you have it will be a short time before he walks free.'

John stifled a smile at his boss's ignorance of how interviewing goes. It's like a cat and mouse chase. Good cats bide their time before they pounce, don't jump in straight away.

Walker probably hadn't even noticed he had struck a nerve with Hunter when he mentioned his sister's virginity, John thought.

There was a knock on the interview room door. The P.C. from the front desk opened the door.

'A moment sir.'

John paused the interview tape and the two detectives stepped out.

'Sir, I don't know if you heard earlier we had a jumper at Ardrossan station. Dead I am afraid.'

John and his boss both shook their heads.

'He has been identified as Isaac McDowall.'

'I though he was still in custody,' John said.

'No, I okayed his release earlier this afternoon.'

'You what? Who is running this case?'

'Technically you might be, but I am your superior.'

Not for the first time John Rose wished he could punch his "superior" and he would have if he could get away with it.

'We still have his statement,' the D.I. said, as if triumphant.

'What? Don't you realise without McDowall's testimony we have one man's word against another's. With nobody there for the defence to cross-examine then the jury will almost definitely side with Hunter who will no doubt now implicate McDowall. The way it stands we really need to hope we get DNA on the baseball bat, or we won't have much of a case,' John said.

A week later John was in his office when his mobile rang. It was Walker.

'We've got him. Fisher's DNA was on the baseball bat. Warrants are out and Paisley Police are assisting by arresting him again.

I am arranging a press conference for tomorrow.'

'Oh, well I won't be able to attend. I am getting dental work done.'

He wasn't, but John would have preferred root canal surgery to being at a press conference with D.I. Walker.

'You have to be there, you solved a case that's been unsolved for 22 years, it should be highlighted.'

'No, sir, I won't be involved in that. You don't get it, do you?'

'Get what?'

'Basically, we will just be highlighting the incompetence of those who came before us. Imagine how you would fell that if after you have retired somebody highlighted a mistake you made.'

'That wouldn't happen with me,' Walker said smugly.

For once John had to agree with him, you needed to make decisions to make mistakes.

'The other thing is if your success on this case is highlighted there could be a promotion in the offing. A move back to the CID squad.'

'Well, it's too late for that. I only have 1 year before I retire so if I get promoted it will look like some kind of sympathy thing. No, if I can stay doing cold cases on my own I will be happy enough doing that.'

CASE 2: The Mullin family. Family of 5 murdered as they slept by an arson attack.

Gibson Crescent, Kilmarnock. May 15th 2003.

TUESDAY, MAY 15th 2003.

Gibson Crescent, Kilmarnock.

Gary 'Jaffa' Gaffney and Malcolm 'Malky' Hood were walking through the deserted Kilmarnock streets, armed with a can of petrol and malice on their minds.

'Jaffa, is this safe?'

'Don't be daft. We are just going to shove a wet rag with petrol on it in this guy's letter box and light it. Just blow a bit of smoke up his arse the boss said. This guy owes a lot of money, we need to set an example, or all these junkies will be wanting their gear for nothing.'

'Here Jaffa, I've a better idea, see the wheely bins.'

'Of course, I've seen them, Malky, we've been walking past the bloody things all the way down the street. Bin day tomorrow, obviously.'

'No, what I mean is see if we get one and stick it against the front door of his flat and light it. Imagine his face when he opens his front door and his bins ablaze. Oh man, that will be so funny.'

The two men laughed at the thought.

'What house is it, Jaffa?'

'It's the third house on the left. Upstairs flat. They are 4 in a block like your mother's street.'

They stopped across the road and surveyed the scene. Two a.m. and every flat along the street was in darkness.

'Right, we will use a wheely bin but will need to carry it,' Jaffa relented.

'Why, it's got wheels. That's why it's called a wheely bin.'

'Oh, and what if the stuff in the bin rattles about and wakes up half the neighbourhood.'

'Good thinking, my man,' Malky said as he realised his mate was always thinking ahead.

They crossed the road quietly and grabbed an end of a bin each. It was surprisingly easy to lift.

'It's half empty,' Jaffa whispered when they placed it outside the flat's door and looked inside, no doubt the reason why it was so easy to carry.

'Hold on, the one across the road must have got a washing machine or something. There's packaging sticking out of theirs.'

Malky rushed away and returned with armfuls of polythene and polystyrene which he placed carefully in the bin until it was running over.

They manoeuvred the bin next to the door at an angle, jammed it in with a planter which had dead looking pansies in it, and put a bit of wood in the letterbox to jam it open.

Malky dropped the contents of a plastic tub of petrol onto the polythene, dropped the bottle in then threw a match in from arm's length. The first match failed to catch but the second caught with a whoosh as the accelerant exploded into life sending flames onto the flat's door.

'Christ, that nearly took the hairs off my arm,' Malky said, louder than he wanted.

'Come on, we will nip out the back and watch,' Jaffa said.

At the bottom of the garden was a wrought iron and wooden bench and they sat down and smoked cigarettes, waiting and watching for frantic activity from the flat above.

While enjoying their second tabs, there was still with no sign of activity from the upstairs flat, but the downstairs neighbour's back door opened, flooding their backdoor with light and sending a barking dog bouncing down their garden and letting the 2 lads know he sensed them. It's loud yapping echoing in the still night.

The two men hid the lighted ends of their ciggies so they could not be seen in the darkness.

'Sheba, stop that barking!' the owner shouted, making more noise than the dog.

Gary and Malcolm sat like statues, hardly daring to breath.

The dog had made its way to the bottom of the garden near where they were sitting, only a wooden fence between them and it's barking and more vicious and louder. Although they hadn't seen the hound the guys thought it sounded savage and hoped it stayed its side of the fence.

'Miaow!' Malky suddenly articulated in what was probably the worst cat impression his mate had ever heard. Jaffa sat beside him, stifling a laugh that would have caused them serious trouble if the neighbours had heard it.

The owner's wife had appeared on the doorstep and was not happy.

'Simon, get that bloody dog in, now. Christ, you will waken the neighbours.'

'It's a bloody cat,' her man said then stomped down the garden to grab the offending mutt.

The two fire starters sat in silence until the shower next door disappeared inside and a few moments later their kitchen light went out.

'Come on, let's go,' Jaffa said, giving the flat one final look before slipping through the privet hedge at the bottom of the garden.

From their vantage point all seemed the same at the flat but unknown to Jaffa and Malky the fire in the bin was raging and had already burnt a hole in the flat's door and was spewing toxic smoke and gas up the stairs and into the flat above.

MONDAY, 16th JUNE 2022

Saltcoats Police Headquarters

Detective Sergeant John Rose made it into the station just before 9 o'clock, later than usual. He pondered why it was when you were running late everything transpired to slow you down even further.

Lex Donnan was on duty at the front desk. She always gave him a warm smile when he passed. Today's smile though seemed contrived, he thought. What she said to him next just proved his theory correct.

'Your boss wants to see you first thing.'

'Who?'

'D.I. Walker.'

'Walker. Is it still Walker?' he asked joking. Detective Inspector Walker had been his line manager for just more than a month, about a month too long as far as he was concerned. Every Monday he said the same to whoever was on the front desk knowing that one week he would be correct.

Lex just smiled. 'Yes, it's still Walker.'

John knocked Walker's office door and entered when invited.

'Take a seat,' his boss said before looking at the clock on the wall. It was after 10 past 9.

'That can't be right,' John said and made a show of checking his own watch, trying to make a joke of it. It was at the same time.

The D.I. wasn't impressed at his attempt at humour.

'Sorry, sir, I had an urgent call to make.'

'Must have been important, if it was more important than coming to see me,' he said sarcastically.

Walker shook his head gently then handed John an old file.

'Your next case, the Mullin family. In 2003 the whole family were killed when somebody set fire to a wheely bin that was placed at their front door.'

John knew all about the case. As a beat cop back then he was seconded to the Kilmarnock force along with 7 other officers. He wasn't going to admit to that to his boss.

'It was obviously huge back then, but nothing has ever been progressed. We have some DNA and fingerprints but no hits when they tried running them,' Walker said with his annoying superior tone.

'Okay sir, I will give it my best shot.'

'I am sure you will. Oh, and keep me in the loop this time.'

John had a habit of forgetting about keeping his boss up to date with whatever developments were happening on any particular case he was working.

Back in his office John fired up his computer to refresh his memory. Somewhere at the back of his mind from back when he was working the case there was a thought among the investigators that it was a case of the wrong flat being torched but it was never made public.

"Police seek wheely bin killers," "Family torched by human rubbish," "Wheely bin killers sought.'

John remembered the newspaper headlines at the time. It was the worst case he had worked on even 20 odd years later. The whole Mullin family perished that fateful night, wiped out as they slept.

As he sat at his desk he put the first fingers of both hands to his eyes and when he put them down they were wet with tears. All the officers who worked the case that month were at their funeral. His abiding memory was looking down from the balcony where he was seated and saw the 5 coffins laid out. The 2 adult boxes, the middle-sized teenager's coffin and the two white coffins, tiny looking from his spot up on the gallery. All containing the family murdered by some evil person or persons.

The memory of those small coffins haunted him for years and he would sure this would prompt those visions to return.

Normally the cases John took on became personal, this would be more than that.

Back to the case and he knew the initial notes would tell him nothing new. The notes they were given back in the day covered all that was in the first file Walker had given him. The only thing he didn't know was the evidence they had, an oil can that had contained the petrol which supplied a couple of smudged prints and the stubs of 4 roll-up cigarettes, found at the bottom of the garden which gave them DNA that still hadn't been traced.

There was only one way forward for John and the way he worked. He would need to go back where it all began, Gilbert Crescent in Kilmarnock. John knew dragging through all those memories would be painful, but he knew he had to do it- for the case.

John parked round the street from the house on Gilbert Crescent. Before he got out of the car he felt a pain in his chest, but it wasn't a physical pain.

Walking down the road he noticed looking at the block where the Mullins had lived, it was obvious the old block of 4 flats had been knocked down and a new block had been built. After all, who would want to stay in the house where probably the most horrendous loss of innocent life in Scotland had been distinguished?

At the time the heinous crime affected everybody. Businesses, the local community and even the criminal underworld rallied to try to get to the bottom of who could be behind it.

Weeks later a local man, Donny Bremner, was charged and taken to court nearly a year later. He lived directly across from the Mullin family and Tam Mullin, the father of the family, had been at his door on more than one occasion accusing him of being a voyeur, staring straight across at his house.

The court decision was unproven, and Bremner walked free. From what D.S. Rose remembered it was a blow to the force who were sure they got their man. Or maybe they were unhappy not to get any man for it, guilty or not.

John Rose walked down the street on the same side where the Mullin's house stood. At the end of the road, he crossed over and walked back slowly, looking into gardens and at houses as he went.

When he reached the block directly opposite what had been the Mullin's he opened the metal gate and walked into the flat where Bremner had lived.

Before he could even close the gate behind him a voice was aimed at him.

'They ain't in!'

He turned and found the front door to the downstairs flat open and an old fat woman balanced on a walking stick and looked at him through thick bottle glass specks. They had a goldfish bowl effect and her eyes looked huge behind the glass.

'Oh, right,' John replied and continued walking in order to talk to the woman without raising his voice.

'Are you a bailiff? I think they have done a runner.'

John shook his head and continued walking towards the old dear. He didn't want to shout his business for all and sundry to hear.

When he reached her he showed her his identity pass.

'I am Detective Sergeant John Rose. I am investigating the cold case killing of the Mullin family.'

The woman crossed herself and muttered something to herself.

'He doesn't live there now,' she said, nodding up towards what had been the Donny Bremner's flat.

'May he rot in Hell,' she added.

'He wasn't found guilty.'

'The system is crooked son. How can a waster, and druggy like him afford a top lawyer? That was how he got off. He bloody did it.'

'Why? Just because Mister Mullin thought he was some kind of peeping tom?'

'No, it was because he touched his older daughter. Dirty pervert, that's what he was.'

The old lady made a face that said he didn't just touch her.

John was surprised at this comment. He had followed the court case back when Bremner was being tried and that was never mentioned.

'Did Tam Mullin assault him then?'

The old woman looked past John and up and down the street to see if anybody might be listening before saying any more.

'Yes, I heard it all. The boy ended up in hospital.'

'When was this, you know, before the fire across the street?'

'Oh, must have been a couple of weeks.'

'Right, missus, thanks for your help.'

'Help?'

'Oh yes, you have been a big help.'

This put a whole new complexion on the events back then, John thought. If there had been a sexual assault why had it not been used in court? Something else for John to look into.

One thing was for certain, John needed to talk to Donny Bremner.

DONNY

Back at his desk he quickly looked up Donny Bremner's record. He had a few warnings as a juvenile for petty vandalism but nothing at all else until he was charged with the 5 charges of murder.

His latest address was in the Kincaidston area of Ayr. Obviously he had moved from the Kilmarnock area and started a new life some 15 or so miles away.

It also said he worked as a painter and decorator and the firm's name. Obviously some of John's predecessor's still thought Bremner was guilty of the Mullin's murder and thought it best to keep tabs on him.

John planned to visit Mister Bremner early the next morning.

As he drove home the facts he had learned that day rattled about in his head. The fact that there were 4 cigarette stubs left at the back of the flats pointed to somebody watching their handy work. Two sets of DNAs so two cigarettes each.

Next morning John Rose drove to Ayr parked up near Bremner's last known address. He walked past the house just before 8 o'clock the next morning. There was a couple of lights on. Chance was he was getting ready for work. He headed round to the rear of the house and saw he didn't have a car or van so he either walked to work or was picked up in the works van.

John hoped it was the former as he planned to intercept him as Donny walked to work.

John got back in his car and watched the street. He had checked the internet the previous day and saw newspaper images of Donny going into court but that was nearly 20 years previously.

Half an hour later a guy who looked to be in his 40's and wearing white overalls walked out of the street John was watching. The white overalls looked paint splattered, this must be his man he thought.

John started the car and drove to catch up with his target. Driving past he stopped and slid the window down.

'Donny!' he called as the guy walked past. He was taking no notice of the car until his name was called.

'Can I have a quick word?'

Donny stopped and walked back and looked in. Straight away he knew John was a policeman. His shoulders drooped and he rubbed his brow.

'What now?'

John showed him his identity card.

'I am D.S. John Rose. I am doing a cold case inquiry into the Mullins killings.'

'Oh, for Christ's sake, not again. I had nothing to do with it. Jesus, I was cleared. Have I not suffered enough. I had to leave Kilmarnock because of it.'

'I know but listen to me first. I don't think you had anything to do with it either. Right. But I do think you can help me solve it. Please, give me 5 minutes. Surely after all your suffering you would like to be cleared once and for all.'

Donny still didn't make a move to get in the car.

'Or we can do it at the Police station,' John added, knowing that would probably be the last thing he wanted to do.

Donny looked to the sky then reluctantly got in. He put his work bag in the well of the car and sat back then crossed his arms.

'What do you want to know?'

'Tell me your story from the start. About why Tam Mullin beat you up. Or before that if it helps.'

'Right, well I was a fitter and worked at an engineering firm. I lived in the flat with my girlfriend, we had been there about 6 months. Then a few months before the fire I was out in the town with Lorraine. She suggested we try drugs. All her pals had tried coke and said it was brilliant. That was the word she used, brilliant.

So, we got some coke and snorted it. She got a nosebleed and that put her off it. Me, I got hooked. I was losing everything. She left me, I lost my job, and I owed a lot of money to my dealer.

Anyway, the night Mullin battered me I walked down the street with his daughter. I just happened to be walking down the road at the same time as her. I asked her how she was doing at school, or something like that. That was all.

Later that night I heard footsteps coming up the stairs. Mullin had let himself in. I never locked the door. By that time, I nothing left to steal, I had sold just about all I had that was worth anything.

I thought it was somebody the dealer sent to warn me and was prepared for that, not for Mullin.

He stormed into the living room. He was like a raging bull. Said I had shagged his daughter and just set about me. I blacked out and woke up in hospital 2 days later.

When I got out I was stuck in bed for a week. The night of the fire I was still going about in crutches. I told the police that at the time, but they wouldn't listen.'

'Who was your dealer?' John asked.

'I got all my gear from a wee toerag called Drew Robinson.'

The name meant nothing to John. He knew that the Robinson guy would just be the end of the line as far as the drug supply was concerned.

'Who is the Mister Big?'

Donny looked down at his hands and was quiet for a minute.

'Will I need to go to court, you know as a witness?'

'No,' John said straight away but he knew that could change, depending on how the rest of the investigation went.

'It was an open secret that the guy at the top of the tree was Andrew Kennedy, you know the taxi guy.'

'The Kennedy from Kennedy's Kabs?'

'Yes. He's pretty much legit now but he made all his money from drugs back then.'

That was a surprise to the D.S., Kennedy Kabs was the biggest taxi operation in Kilmarnock and Andrew could be seen on the Scottish Television most nights extolling the virtues of TV while promoting his business.

'Thanks for that Donny, that was all I needed to know. This is my card, if you think of anything else that might help me, give me a call, okay.'

Donny reluctantly took the card from him and stuck it in the top pocket of his overalls.

'Where are you going just now, I will drop you off,' the Policeman offered.

'No, it's okay, I get picked up at the end of the road.'

Just at that they were blinded by a van approaching which had its light on at full beam.

'That's my lift. I will need to go back to the house to get them.'

Donny opened the door and got out. As he reached back in to get his work bag John Rose stuck a hand out.

'Donny, I am glad you have turned things around. Good luck in the future.'

'Thanks,' Donny said as he shook the hand. Then he grabbed the bag and hurried back to get his lift.

'Andrew Kennedy, I think I need a word with you next' John said to himself before he drove off heading for home. His stomach was groaning as he hadn't managed anything to eat before he left early that morning.

Karen, his wife, was phoned as he neared Irvine and an order for brunch put in.

Karen was putting the finishing touches to John's fry-up when John got home. The smell in the kitchen added to his need for food and he sat at the table and started eating a bit of toast while Karen plated up the rest of his food.

'What are the flowers for?' John asked.

In the middle of the kitchen table there was a bunch of flowers stuck in a vase, but the polythene was still on them.

'I bought them for you to take to the Mullin's grave.'

John had only mentioned the case the night before because he was getting up early the next day to speak to Donny Bremner. He hadn't expected her to go and get flowers that morning, but it would be a nice touch.

Back when it happened the fire and loss of the whole Mullin family had affected everybody who heard about it. Most folk reflected on how they would feel if a whole branch of their family's died. Absolutely devastating, no doubt.

John placed the bunch of flowers in the boot of his unmarked Police car. He was heading for Kilmarnock Cemetery. He should probably have gone there when he visited the Mullin's house earlier, but the flowers prompted him to do it now.

Although he had attended the service for the Mullin family he hadn't gone to the cemetery for the internment. He hoped he could find the grave easily enough.

There again it was a nice morning and a stroll around the graveyard wasn't the worst thing he could be spending a bit of time doing. Especially when he had a bellyful of food to walk off.

The cemetery was quiet. Quiet as a graveyard in fact. Save for some birdsong from several feathered friends in the ancient trees.

John had never been in the graveyard before and ambled up and down the lanes checking names and dates. As he walked he held the flowers with their blooms face down and at his side. Carrying a bunch of flowers was alien to him. Even though he was alone in the graveyard he still felt uneasy walking around with a bunch of blooms.

When he found the Mullin's grave it was plain to see no expense had been spared on the headstone. It was the largest on the row by a margin as the family had 2 adjoining lairs with only 3 casks allowed in each one. The memorial stone was black marble with gold lettering.

John read the inscription: Mullin. Together forever. Thomas (Tam) 1970-2003 Martha 1974-2003 Brittany 1990-2003 Jack 2000-2003 Lily 2002-2003.

Seeing the names laid out like that hit John harder than even he thought it would or could. He wiped a tear from his eyes then set about sorting his flowers. Now he wanted to get it done and walk away.

There was a bunch of dried stalks in the flower rose that John took out. The bunch of flowers looked too small in the flower holder, it was obviously family sized, like the stone but he wasn't going to get more flowers to fill it.

John stood back and nodded to the graves in respect. As he looked up he noticed the gravestone next to theirs was a tiny plain stone with the simple inscription: Malcolm Hood 1976-2003.

The irony that the murdered family were buried next to a hood wasn't lost on John.

As John walked away he worked out his next move. He couldn't just turn up at Andrew Kennedy's place without liaising with the CID in Kilmarnock first. If he was a known drug dealer there might be an ongoing investigation regarding him. If he blundered into that his neck, or other parts of his body, would be on the line.

He would need to get permission from his boss, D.I. Walker, who would in turn get John the authorisation he needed. In order to do that he would need to get his report up to date, something Walker had reprimanded him about before. Back to Saltcoats and the computer.

WALKER

John got back to his office after 2 o'clock and spent more than an hour writing up his notes, the part of the job he hated. Although he liked working on his own at times he missed a colleague who was good at writing up notes.

When he finished he tried phoning his boss but the D.I.'s phone was constantly engaged. As the clock ticked close to 4 o'clock John decided to go to his office.

Looking in he saw his boss sitting at his computer with headphones on, no doubt in an important zoom call.

After about 5 minutes he saw John standing outside his office door. He scribbled something on a sheet of paper and held it up where John could see it. Email me was all it said.

John stormed away, getting more pissed off by the second with his boss. A thought came to him: if the Roman's thought that an army marched on its stomach then it was pretty obvious now that a modern Police force prevaricates on its computer.

He switched his computer on again and typed what he needed and when, that being asap, as in first thing the next morning because he wanted to be heading to Kilmarnock sooner rather than later.

John sat in front of his computer, surfing the web, finding out as much as he could about Andrew Kennedy. The Kennedy Kab's owner was a fan of publicity and more so self-publicity. There were dozens of local newspaper articles of him donating to various charities. As they went back in time he was getting younger looking but always narcissistic.

Between times John would stop and check his inbox of his email, without success, waiting for a message back from Walker.

After a while John had surfed back to 2003 and there he was, Kennedy, black suited in mourning and offering, on behalf of a collection of local businesses, a reward of £10,000 for information leading to the arrest of the person or people responsible for the murder of the Mullin family. John smiled at the irony, it looked the way his investigation was going that Kennedy was confident the reward wouldn't be getting paid out.

Then John wondered if he would be eligible to collect that money if he solved the mystery that had eluded the Police for 19 years before him.

John checked his email again and found no reply from Walker. Then he saw it was just gone 5 o'clock. He wouldn't still be on a zoom meeting after finishing time at 5. John switched off his computer and locked his office before heading back down to catch his boss before he disappeared for the night.

The office was in darkness and the door was locked when he tried it.

'What a useless,' John said before biting his tongue. He got out his mobile phone and called the D.I.

It was answered after 5 rings and Walker's whiney voice could be heard above the noise of traffic. No doubt he was in his car, heading home.

'Detective Inspector Walker here.'

'Yes, sir, it's D.S. Rose here, I wondered if you had a chance to read the report I sent you.'

'No, I am sorry John. I was on a zoom call until I finished.'

'It's just that I am in a hurry to progress this investigation and I need to liaise with Kilmarnock C.I.D.'

'John, the case is 19 years old. Another few hours or days won't make a difference, will it?'

'It will to me sir. I want to get on with this investigation.'

'Okay, I will read it first thing tomorrow and contact you to arrange a meeting.'

'Okay sir, you enjoy your night,' John said, through gritted teeth, before cutting the call.

Next day and John's disclination of D.I. Walker had grown. People who didn't share his drive and work ethic exasperated him. Next time he spoke with him it would take all his self-restraint to not hit him.

Sure, the case was nearly 20 years old, but the family and friends of the Mullin family had been grieving all that time and searching for answers. Walker hadn't seen those tiny coffins in the church containing the bodies of babies whose lives were cruelly taken. He didn't wake up in the middle of the night and lie staring at the ceiling wishing he could have done more to solve their murders all those years ago, even though he was a mere flat foot working on the beat on the periphery of the case.

John spent the morning looking further into Andrew Kennedy and the rapid rise of Kennedy Kabs. The problem John knew would be Kennedy would have been at the top of the proverbial drugs tree back then but was a legit businessman now and would no doubt just lawyer up if he got too close to what he wanted to know.

By the time his boss phoned him his wrath toward him had dimmed a bit. His resolve to nail Kennedy hadn't. In fact, it had grown intensely.

'John, I have contacted Kilmarnock CID and they will be glad to help you. If you report tomorrow at 10 o'clock they will be expecting you. Oh, and good work. Excellent report.''

'Thank you sir,' he said, again through gritted teeth,' before killing the call.

CAIRNS

John Rose rocked up to the Kilmarnock Police station at 10 to 10 the next morning. The front desk was unoccupied, and he rang for attention. He thought about ringing it again, but he clearly heard a muffled ringing from the bell in the back room, and he knew they must have heard it.

It was a full 2 minutes before a young P.C. appeared. John flashed his card, explained who he was and asked for the CID. The young guy looked a bit bemused but left and went to the back office.

A few minutes later a young D.C. appeared through from the CID area.

John explained it all again, but the young cop didn't know of any arrangement but took him through to the CID area.

It wasn't exactly a hive of activity, but he was invited to wait while the young officer went for help.

All the time the D.S. couldn't help but think his boss had screwed it up.

Eventually a guy of about his own age appeared from the floor above.

'John? I am D.S. Donald Cairns. I've been asked to help you.'

He then offered a fist pump, a sign that he felt Covid wasn't away yet. John reciprocated awkwardly, not his style. He was an old-fashioned handshake kind of guy.

'Come on up to my office and we can talk there.'

'Have you been told why I am here?' John asked.

'No, just that you need our assistance.'

John shook his head. Fucking great, he thought, Walker couldn't even pass on any of the details of what he needed, that would have let Donald get some background done for him.

John followed Donald, thinking as he went that this guy was probably the Kilmarnock equivalent of himself, nearing retirement and used to backfill for others or given menial tasks to fill his shifts.

Donald's office was much like his own, a converted cupboard with the bare essentials, computer, table and filing stuff. There were 2 chairs that practically filled the floor space.

'So, what is it you do here, Donald?' John asked.

'Burglary specialist they are calling me now. I have to collate all the burglaries in the past year and collect together those with the same or a similar m.o.. What about you?'

'Cold case murders. I am working on the Mullin murders from 2023.'

Donald never spoke but his eyes told John he knew the significance of the case.

'Were you involved back then?' John asked.

'Yes, I think everyone at the station was in one way or another.'

'Me too. I was seconded with a few others from Saltcoats.'

'So, why are you looking into the case? Are they trying to say we were incompetent here in Kilmarnock?'

'It might be what our bosses want but that's the last thing I would do. I told my boss that when I took this new role on. I solved the Colin Fisher case recently. You know, the lad from Crosshouse who was killed after a night out.

I don't think it cast a shadow over the previous enquiries although there were more holes in the investigation than a Swiss cheese.'

'I heard there was an arrest. Was it not some guy Walker that broke the case?'

'My boss. I let him take the kudos, keeps me clean.'

'Before we start, do you fancy a coffee?'

'I'd love a tea.'

'Right, take a pew and I will be back in 2 minutes. What do you take in your tea?'

'Milk and 2 sugars, ta.'

John sat and looked at the large map of Kilmarnock and surrounding area Donald had on the wall hat is it you in front of his desk. It was populated with different coloured pins, and it looked quite impressive with a key at the side stating what kind of burglaries they were. John thought the guy had the same kind of work ethic as himself and felt they could get on.

Donald arrived back with the drinks and sat beside John.

'What's your story Donald, this looks like a converted cupboard?'

Donald looked round his less than salubrious surroundings.

'Unfortunately, it would seem to some that I am regarded as some kind of dinosaur. A non-conformist and a bit of a troublemaker.'

John laughed. 'I wonder if there is one of us in every station.'

Donald laughed too. 'You too eh. They are trying to force me to retire but it won't work.'

'Snap.'

'Is that why you are on the cold cases then, John?'

'Yes. I think they thought it would just keep me out of the way, but this is my second case, and I solved the first one. I am sure my bosses will now be claiming it was a stroke of genius.'

'So, what is it you need from us?'

'Well, I want to interview Andrew Kennedy.'

'Any Andrew Kennedy in particular? I am sure there could be a dozen in Kilmarnock.'

'Thee Andrew Kennedy, the Kennedy Kabs one.'

'Oh, him.' Donald looked surprised. 'What for?'

'The guy the force tried to set up for the murder of the Mullin's, Donny Bremner, was a heavy drugs user at the time and Andrew Kennedy was his dealer.'

'Kennedy was a drug dealer?'

Donald's look showed he was heavy surprised.

'Oh, he might be legit now but back then he was the main dealer in Kilmarnock. Come on Donald don't come the innocent. We have been in the game long enough not to be bullshitting each other.'

'Yes you are right, we knew he was the main dealer, but he kept himself squeaky clean.'

It wasn't what he said but the way he said it had John's detective sense tingling.

'Donald, there must have been more to it than that. Back then if they couldn't get him legally there would have been trumped up charges to get at him. Come on, be honest with me. If we are going to work together we need to be honest with each other.'

Donald Cairns got up and walked over and opened the office door and looked out furtively to check the coast was clear. He sat back down before speaking again.

'He was a grass. Gave information that led to the arrests of a lot of nasty people. He also had people in high places looking after him until he got his taxi business established then went legit.'

'Funny how they couldn't nail the Mullin's killer at the time.'

'Word was he dealt with it.'

'What does that mean?'

Donald put his hand out, showing that he didn't know what it meant either.

'All the more reason that I would want to speak to him.'

'Are you sure?'

'Yes. What I want to know now then is who his known accomplices were then? Who did his supplying, right down to his runners. I am sure 2 of his guys did this.'

'That is probably a need-to-know basis,' Donald said.

'Well, right now, I need to know.'

'Okay, wait here.'

Donald left and John sat for a minute twiddling his thumbs before studying the map in front of him closely. It only kept his attention for a few minutes. Next he opened one of the drawers on Donald's desk and pulled out a folio. It was the ongoing investigations in the Kilmarnock area and made interesting reading, even though the crimes weren't even in his neck of the woods.

Flasher exposing himself to teenage girls. Teenagers being robbed for their mobile phones. Suspected people trafficking in the area. Hit and run driver sought.

Hearing footsteps he closed the file and quickly slipped it back in the drawer.

Donald sat down then pulled a piece of paper from his inside pocket. It had a dozen names on it.

'I didn't give you this and nothing on it can be used as evidence, right.'

'Right.'

John quickly scanned it although he didn't know who or what he was looking for, but one name stood out. Malcolm Hood. Where did he know that name from, he wondered.

Then it clicked, the small headstone next to the Mullin's grave.

'Who is this Malcolm Hood?'

'Who was he? Committed suicide. Jumped from a motorway flyover onto the path of an oncoming lorry. He was a small time heavy, not the brightest.'

'Could that be how Kennedy dealt with it? Did they do an autopsy to check if he was dead before he left the flyover?'

'As far as I remember the lorry hit him at about 60 miles per hour. Not much left to autopsy after that.'

'Or you didn't want to do it. Not you specifically, I mean.'

'You might be right, but we will never know.'

'I still want to talk to Kennedy. The reason I came to Kilmarnock CID was in case there were any other ongoing investigations involving him, didn't want to tread on anyone else's toes.'

'Right, leave it with me, give me your number and I will get back to you.'

'When?'

'Later today.'

John hadn't made an effort to get up and looked at Donald.

'One way or another I will phone you today,' D.S. Cairns promised.

John took his card out of his wallet and handed it over.

'Thanks, Donald. I think we could make a good team. We could get results.'

'Or get us sacked,' Donald said with a wry smile.

KENNEDY

Donald phoned later that afternoon and gave John the all clear. They were to meet at Kennedy's taxi premises at an industrial estate on the outskirts of Kilmarnock the next morning at 11 o'clock to meet the man himself.

John was there early, checking out what he could of the operation. The front of the huge unit was furnished the same as all the other units. Dark wooden frames on an insipid grey concrete rendered building only his was different, a huge garishly coloured "Kennedy Kabs" sign in 8-foot multi-coloured letters topped the roof. Industrial chic it wasn't.

John walked round the back and found it was a hive of activity. Mechanics working on cars, checking engines and tyres, smartly dressed drivers cleaning their cars for the shifts ahead. The noise of industrial hoovers filled the air.

When John walked back to the front of the building Donald was parking up.

John waited until his new partner got out and was welcomed by another fist pump.

'How are we going to do this?' Donald asked.

'I am quite happy to do the talking. Feel free to jump in if you have a point to make.'

They entered the building and were immediately assaulted by a large frame of Kennedy himself, a photograph of him with a disabled guy receiving a cheque for 5 grand.

The corridor went to the left, but John noticed the door to the right had a huge padlock on it, much more than he would have expected for inside a unit like that. Outside maybe, but not inside.

Walking along the corridor the walls festooned with a gallery of pictures, each one showing Andrew Kennedy in some charitable guise. Even dressed as Santa but without the beard of course, you had to see it was him. John had never met such an egotistical man, if the gallery was anything to go by.

As they walked down the corridor a muffled voice could be heard on the phone. The call was ended abruptly as they reached the doorway.

The office door was open, and Andrew ushered them in, smiling as he did so. The smile as false as his dark hair colour.

He proffered a hand across his large desk and the two officers took turns shaking. John was surprised Donald hadn't opted for a fist pump.

'Hello gents, how can I be of service? Is it a charitable matter?'

'No, I am afraid it's a Police matter,' John said.

'Well, as I said, how can I be of service?'

Kennedy was a slight guy, possibly in his 50's or more the age deceptive because of the dark brown hair colour, thanks obviously to product control. His eyes, as he looked from one cop to the other were piercing green.

John thought he had snake eyes that at the moment were looking to see which of the two would be his prey. John decided to attack like a mongoose.

'I am looking into the murder of the Mullin family in 2003.'

Theatrically Kennedy put one hand to his face, the other reaching out, as if he was in pain.

'A terrible thing,' he said, his voice sounding almost tearful.

'What was your involvement?'

'Along with a few other local businessmen we offered a reward,' he said, switching to charity champion, keeping the sad face.

'No, I mean by the fact that you were Donny Bremner's drug supplier and I reckon the firebomb warning was meant for him.'

'Me a drug dealer?' He put on an utterly flabbergasted look, as if John's claim was the craziest thing he had ever heard.

'Donald, are you going along with this folly?'

'John is the investigating officer,' Donald said, leaving John a bit on his own, not exactly backing him.

'Mister Kennedy, I know you are a busy businessman so let's cut the crap. We all know you made your money from dealing in drugs and now you are a legitimate businessman. We can take this conversation down to the station or we can carry it on now.'

Andrew Kennedy's attitude changed quite dramatically. He stared straight at John now, his eyes narrowed and were now python-like as he looked as if he was prepared to strike at his prey. He stared John out before he spoke.

'Supposing, just supposing, what you say is true, I could not say I ordered anyone to firebomb this Bremner guy or anybody else. That would be wrong.'

'Would your dealers or their runners take it upon themselves to give somebody who owed them a lot of money a little frightener off their own backs.'

'Any business, whether it be what you would call legitimate or illegal can only survive if incomings are greater than outgoings. If my drivers gave free hires they wouldn't be driving for long. I would encourage them to use legal ways to ensure they are paid and if I found out they were using illegal methods they wouldn't be working for me. I have a reputation to maintain.'

'Taxiing doesn't really compare to drug dealing but I know what you are saying. There was a rumour back at the time that you caused it, and you sorted it.'

'Yes, a rumour you said. That is all it would be.'

'Was Malcolm Hood responsible?'

'Who?'

'Come on, Andrew, he worked for you back in the day and committed an alleged suicide just over a week after the Mullins were killed.'

Andrew Kennedy sat back in his large leather chair and folded his arms.

'I don't know why you are here because you seem to know all the answers.' Before adding, almost casually, 'or at least think you know the truth.'

To John, his first comment was as good as a confession. He nodded his head as if in agreement but prepared his comeback.

'Who was with him?'

Kennedy lifted his hands up as if feigning ignorance.

'Was it one, two, three guys? Maybe he was on his own. Your guess is as good as mine.'

'Two people were there that night, that's a fact, we have evidence of that.'

Kennedy was non-plussed at the fact.

'I will solve this, with or without your help,' John said.

'I don't know how I could help you. I would if I could.'

'Okay, Andrew, thank you for your help. Now, I will leave you my card. I am based at Saltcoats Police Station. I will be happy to leave here and never see you again if I get a note, anonymously of course, telling me who else was there that night. Just imagine if it was your family, surely you would want justice for the 5 that died that night.'

Andrew got up to his feet to show them out.

'Gents, thanks for your visit and I am sorry I couldn't have helped you more.'

He reached out to shake again but John ignored the offer. The thought of shaking the snake's hand again filled him with dread. Cairns didn't decline the offer.

As they walked down the hallway heading out John looked closely again at the lock on the door in the other half of the unit. It also had a lock and key, definitely security overkill. Especially as the taxi business operated 27/4 and the unit always occupied.

Outside John bumped fists with D.S.Cairns again and thanked him for his help, even though he kind of threw him under a bus with Kennedy.

As they stood talking they couldn't help but notice parked outside the industrial unit and just down the road a bit was what seemed a brand-new Rolls Royce. Impossible to tell the age of the car because the vain Mister Kennedy had a personal plate but certainly wasn't a banger.

They walked down towards it and had a quick look in at the luxury interior.

'What about that, Donald, if you had the money for that you could afford to retire, eh?' John asked.

'Sure, must be worth a couple of hundred grand.'

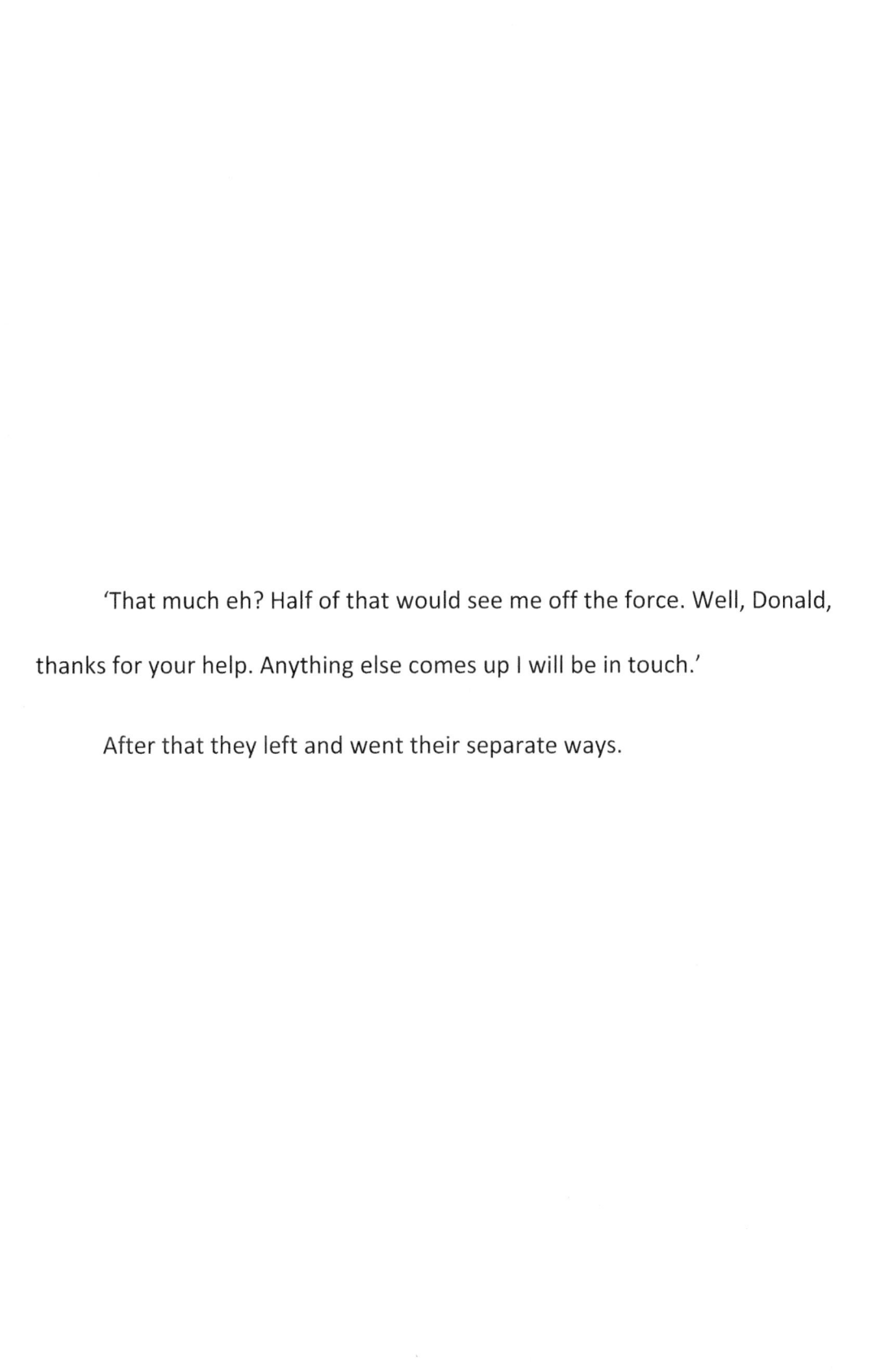

'That much eh? Half of that would see me off the force. Well, Donald, thanks for your help. Anything else comes up I will be in touch.'

After that they left and went their separate ways.

KAREN

The cooking smell that met John when he walked in his front door had his stomach doing somersaults. Karen's home-made steak pie was John's favourite dinner. He wondered what she wanted him to buy her, that was her usual trick.

Twenty minutes later John pushed his plate away; he couldn't eat any more.

Karen looked at the plate that still had some food on it.

'What's wrong, is the food not up to sir's standards?'

'What? No, it was brilliant as ever love.'

'So, what's bothering you?'

'It's the case I am working. I have been reading over some of the case notes again and it's quite harrowing.'

'What is it?'

'You know I can't discuss it.'

'John, you have been saying that for the past 20 years since you joined the Police. I have never asked what you were working on but if you bring it home then maybe it's time you started talking about it. If you are working on your own maybe you just need to get some of it off your chest.'

John looked at his wife. They both knew him talking about a case could jeopardise it and lead to a failed conviction. However, once again he knew she was right. It was too personal to him to keep it bottled up.

'Do you remember the Mullin family whose house was torched back in 2003? They called it the wheely bin killers because they set fire to a wheely bin and stuck it next to their flat's front door.'

'Of course, I remember it. Was that not in Kilmarnock?'

'Yes.'

'I thought they got somebody for that years ago?'

'They did but it was a set up. Hate to say it but the Police needed a conviction, and he was the stool pigeon. The evidence didn't point to him at all, and he was found not guilty.'

'The whole family were wiped out, weren't they?'

John nodded gravely. 'They all died from smoke inhalation. The mother and oldest daughter lived for another 2 days after the fire, but they died too.'

'I remember everybody talking about it at the time, we were all imagining what it would be like if it happened to somebody you knew personally. And their surviving family. God, it doesn't bear thinking about it.'

John speared another bit of steak he had left on his plate and put it in his mouth.

'Have you got any leads, any ideas?'

'Have you heard of Kennedy Kabs in Kilmarnock?'

'Yes. That's the guy on Scottish Television at tea-time. Looks like a right arrogant sod.'

'You are telling me. I met him today. Not a nice person at all. Well, he was a former drug dealer, and I am sure he was behind the fire. Trouble is, back then he was a Police informer and like all clever guys he left no evidence to link himself to the crime.'

'You know honey, there is a well-known stress relief a wife can give her husband. That is, if you are up for it.'

'How can I resist an offer like that?'

Next morning John sat at the kitchen table looking into his cup of tea when Karen walked in. She patted him on the shoulders.

'Don't worry about it, love. It was probably the stress.'

'It doesn't mean I don't love you. I love you more now than I ever did. Every night I want you but then when we finally do it, I can't finish.'

'Look, I told you last night it was okay. I got my pleasure. I am sure if I was doing your job I would be stressed with it.'

'As long as you don't think there is somebody else, you know I would never do that.'

'Of course, I do. You are my faithful hound.'

A NEW WEEK

John Rose walked up to his office with a heavy heart. He felt as though he may have reached the end of the road as far as the Mullin investigation was concerned.

The rest of the previous week, after meeting Kennedy, he had spent alone in his office. He started reading through more of the reports from the initial investigation on the Mullin killings. Nothing new was coming to him. It seemed getting a DNA match for the other cigarette stub was the only way of solving the case. Obviously one belonged to the late Malcolm Hood, but who was his accomplice that night?

His next task was to check through the other names on the list D.S. Cairns had given him of Kennedy's known associates. Again, he drew a blank, none of them had been in trouble with the Police since 2003.

Most, however, were taxi drivers, no doubt working for Kennedy Kabs. That was, of course, if they really were taxi drivers and not muscle being paid by Kennedy and their jobs registered as cabbies. Only, of course, if Kennedy wasn't a completely legitimate businessman.

Nagging at the back of his mind the whole time was the fact he hadn't been able to climax with his wife. Was it stress or just his age? He was only 62, surely he should still be full of seed.

Finally, he turned his attention to Andrew Kennedy. Guys like Kennedy found it hard to go completely straight. Plus, would a taxi business owner, even a very successful one, be able to afford a Rolls Royse like he had? Even if it was second hand it was still worth over a hundred grand.

John also found out he lived in a large mansion which he bought 5 years previously and it had been on the market for half a million when he bought it.

He hadn't long switched on his computer when his mobile rang. Karen's name flashed up and he answered it.

'John, you just got a weird thing in the post.'

'What do you mean weird?'

'It was a card addressed to you and inside was an In Remembrance card and the name on it was Gary Gaffney.'

Straight away John remembered he was on the list of Kennedy's associates from Donald Cairns' list.

'What's it about John?'

'It's a kind of code. The cop I was working with from Kilmarnock couldn't give me the guy's name. It's to do with the Mullin's case.'

It was a good thing he was lying to Karen over the phone, she could usually tell when he was telling her porkies.

'Oh right. Just seemed a bit morbid.'

'Yes, he had a dark sense of humour.'

'Right, love. See you tonight then, love you.'

'Love you too,' he said, as he finished the call.

Kennedy had come through with the other guy's name but exactly in the sort of way John expected, sending it to his home address. It was obviously a sort of "I know where you live threat."

John wasn't scared easy, and this latest thing didn't bother him. In fact, he felt it pointed to Kennedy being behind the Mullins murders but also showed he wasn't the legitimate businessman he made himself out to be.

It also made John all the more determined to nail him.

So, who was Gary Gaffney?

He wasn't, as far as John could find, employed by Kennedy. A google search on his computer found him in a local newspaper with his old boss

Kennedy being presented with a specially adapted wheelchair for his son Richard.

Who could he ask about Gaffney?

After his performance the previous day he felt he couldn't completely trust D.S. Cairns, so who else? Then he remembered D.I. Amy Hammond was from Kilmarnock. He didn't know if she was on duty, he would go down to the detective's offices to see.

John was in luck; Amy was sitting at her desk in her office. He knocked gently on her office door which was open.

She turned and looked surprised to see him.

'Oh, hi John.'

'Amy. You are from Kilmarnock.' She nodded. 'What do you know about Gary Gaffney and his son Richard?'

'They are such a nice couple of guys. Richard was born with a spinal defect and his dad has been his carer for years.'

'So, he doesn't work?'

'No, he is a full-time carer. His wife left when Richard was a baby.'

'Where do they live?'

'It was in the New Farm Loch area last I knew.'

'Thanks.'

'What's this about? If you don't mind me asking.'

'I'm interested in Andrew Kennedy, you know Kennedy Kabs and Gaffney came up as a person of interest.'

'Kennedy? What's this about?'

'I had a meeting with Kennedy regarding an investigation I am running. Something about him didn't run true to me.'

'A murder enquiry?'

John nodded and Amy went on.

'I know what you mean. I was at a charity event a few years ago and he was hosting it. If he was chocolate he would eat himself, but I know what you mean, he seemed a bit of a creep to me.'

'Right, thanks for that. New Farm Loch it is for me, if that is where Gaffney still lives.'

GAFFNEY

John found the Gaffney's address after more searching on the Net; it was still in New Farm. He headed there after lunch, hoping he would be in.

There was what looked like a specially adapted people carrier in the driveway of the house, so chance was he was in, John thought.

He knocked on the door and had his i.d. card on a lanyard round his neck.

Gary opened the door.

'Mister Gaffney, D.S. John Rose from Police Scotland. Mind if I have a word?'

'Sure, come in.'

As John walked into the hallway a teenage boy in the wheelchair, John saw being donated by Kennedy, appeared at the lounge door, keen to see who their visitor was.

'It's the Police Richard, what have you been up to? You haven't been joyriding again,' his father asked jokingly.

Richard smiled. 'Who is Joy?'

All three laughed. Sort of gallows humour you had to have to survive in their position, John guessed.

'I think we should speak in private, Gary,' John said quietly.

'Sure. Richard, best you go through to your room.'

'Right dad. Men talk eh.? Have you been riding Joy?'

'I've not being riding anybody.'

With that he whizzed off down to his room.

'So, what is so private?'

'The Mullin murders in 2003.'

Gary looked at him and swallowed before speaking.

'Best come in and take a seat.'

John sat on the sofa while Gary sat on a leather recliner.

'I'm doing a cold case investigation and I know Malcolm Hood and an accomplice set the fire at the Mullin's house. What can you tell me about it?'

'Nothing, except what I heard at the time. It was Danny Bremner, wasn't it? The guy that lived across the road.'

'You mean Donny Bremner. No. I spoke to Donny; he reckons it was him they were supposed to be giving him a warning and got the wrong house.'

'News to me,' Gary said as he shrugged his shoulders.

'I will tell you why I am here, we have forensic evidence from the Mullin's house. I have a list of Malcolm Hood's known associates from back when he worked with Kennedy's taxis, and we want to do DNA tests on all the people on the list. Would you be willing to give a DNA sample?'

'I don't know. You see I don't trust all that science stuff and as you can see I am Richard's carer. What would happen if I was wrongly identified as being at the house?'

'Gary, science like that is 100% accurate. The only way you would be identified is if you were actually there.'

'I still don't know.'

'Life must be tough for you; I take it you have to be with your son 24/7.'

'Yes, but as you said, it's my son. I am sure you would do the same for your kids.'

'Yes, of course. All the same, it must be very tying.'

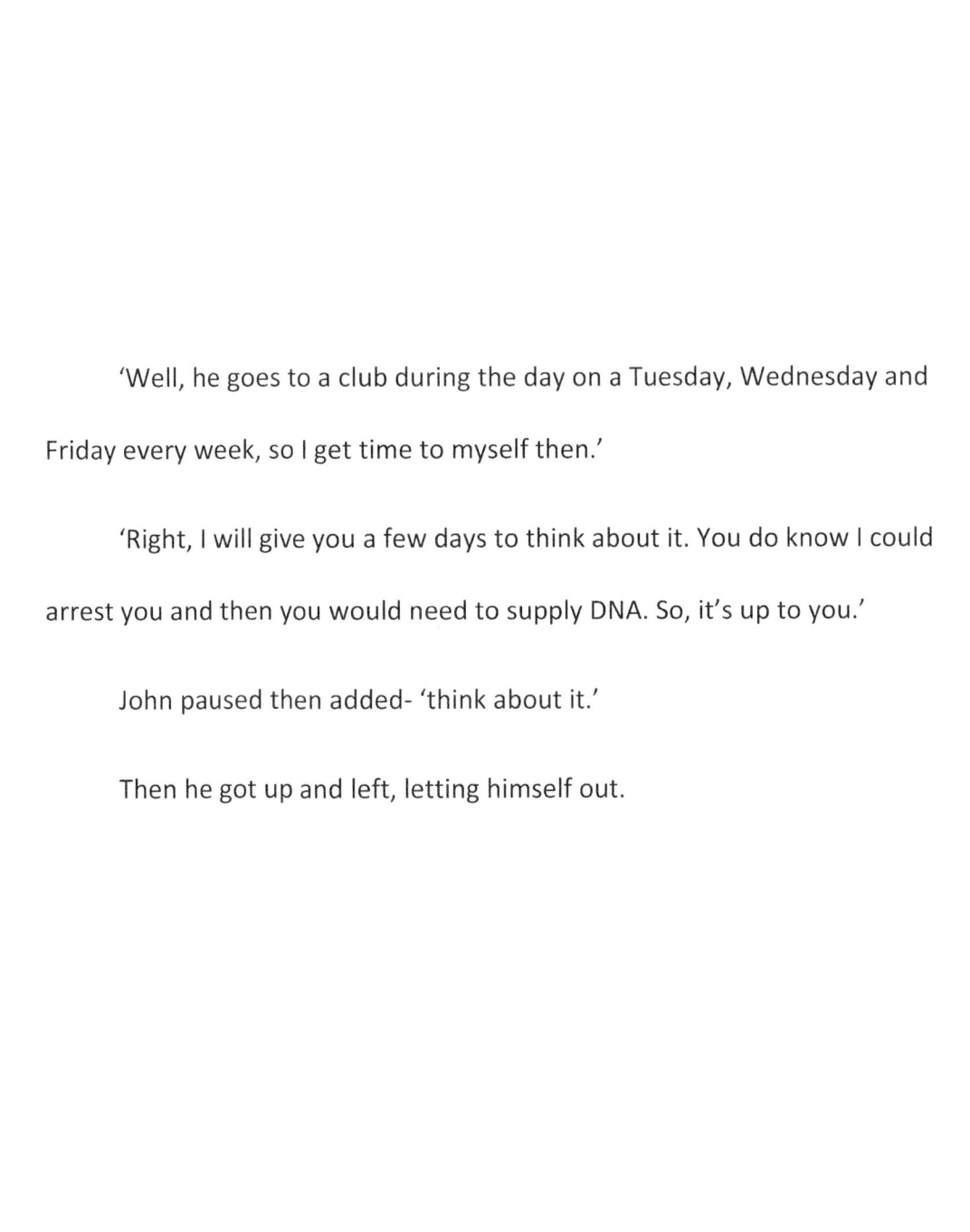

'Well, he goes to a club during the day on a Tuesday, Wednesday and Friday every week, so I get time to myself then.'

'Right, I will give you a few days to think about it. You do know I could arrest you and then you would need to supply DNA. So, it's up to you.'

John paused then added- 'think about it.'

Then he got up and left, letting himself out.

TUESDAY

Next morning John put the next part of his plan into action. He headed off to Kennedy Kab's with a bag full of DNA kits.

He arrived just before 10 o'clock and was pleased to see Kennedy's Roller wasn't parked out front of the unit. If he never met him in person again it would be too soon.

The taxi control room and office was the room opposite Kennedy's own office and John could hear voices, or at least a voice, from within. He knocked gently at first but got no reply.

After trying another twice, he opened the door slowly and looked inside. There was only the one occupant, sitting at a large desk facing him. She motioned him in with a wave as she was talking on the phone through her headset.

John walked forward and waited until she ended the call.

The woman was in her 30's or 40's and looked a bit unkempt. Her hair beneath her headset looked uncombed and was a combination of grey roots and horrible faded yellow hair that had obviously been dyed at home. From where she was sitting his attention couldn't be drawn anywhere else than her more than ample chest that seemed to be trying to escape from her low-cut t-shirt. She had a pretty face that seemed to light up when she smiled.

He flashed his identity card he had round his neck.

'Hi, I am Detective Sergeant John Rose. I am looking into a cold case murder, and I am looking to get DNA samples from some of your staff.'

'Murder,' she said, as the smile slipped from her face. 'You think one of our drivers have committed a murder?'

'No, it's just to eliminate their DNA from our investigation.'

'Oh, right.'

John handed over the list he had printed out, all in alphabetical order.

Before she could say or do anything else the telephone rang.

'I need to take this,' the woman said.

John gave her a thumbs up and she continued with the call.

'Kennedy Kabs. Certainly, your name. He should be with you in 5 minutes madam.'

She then went onto the pressed a button on a mobile phone.

'Albert, Mrs. Jessie Brown, Asda to London Road.'

She looked down the list.

'Derek Allan, he is off duty today. Adam Crawford should be arriving anytime to start his shift. David Easton, he is one of our mechanics, he is in the yard just now. I'll get him in.'

She picked the phone up and called the mechanic to come to the office.

'The only other driver on duty just now is Rod Harvey. I'll give him a call.'

John felt a presence behind him. He looked round to see a small, bald guy wearing a Kennedy Kabs polo shirt.

'Adam, this Policeman would like a word.'

'Yes, sir. Adam is it? I am Detective Constable John Rose and I am working a cold case murder and we are trying to eliminate Kennedy Kabs employees that worked for him in 2003. I take it you haven't given a DNA sample to the Police before?'

'No.'

'Would you be willing to give me a DNA sample?'

'Eh., sure. What do I need to do?'

'I just need to swab inside your mouth then it will be sent away to the lab. As I said it's just a process of elimination.'

John got his test kit out and quickly swabbed Adam.

As he was writing Adam's name and the date on it a burly, greasy looking guy wearing oily overalls appeared at the office door.

The telephonist was back on the phone and John introduced himself and explained what he was doing.

David agreed to take the test too.

After John swabbed him David asked the now free phone woman if that was all she wanted. When she said it was John was left alone with the woman again as Adam had made himself scarce by then.

He tried not to stare at her voluminous breasts, but it was hard not to.

'By the way, you haven't said your name. As I said, I am John.'

'Oh, it's Carol.'

'Oh Carol. Sounds like a song,' John said, smiling as he continued to stare at her, trying to get his view above her golden globes.

Although John's crack wasn't very funny, if it even was funny at all, Carol laughed as if it was the funniest thing she had ever heard. As she laughed her whole body was moving and John was surprised one of her big puppies didn't actually escape from her top.

'You could leave the test things here and I could see that they are all done,' Carol offered when she stopped laughing.

'No, the tests need to be witnessed. Official like, not that I don't trust you but it's obviously an ongoing investigation.'

'Right, I see. Sorry, silly of me.'

There was a knock on the office door and the door opened to reveal Rod Harvey. He was in his 40's but was not the guy John would fancy seeing in a cab late at night. He was over 6 foot, completely bald although he had a tattoo of a snake over the top of his head. He was also ugly, and his only other distinguishing added feature was a dirty scar across the cheek.

'Hi Rod. John is a Policeman and would like you to give a sample for DNA,' Carol said to him.

Rod immediately crossed his arms in defiance but never spoke.

'Hi Rod. I am carrying out a cold case murder investigation and would like all the staff here to give me DNA samples to rule them out.'

'All the staff?'

'No, just most of the ones that have been here since 2003.'

'What if I refuse?'

'Well, the easy way is to do it here. Takes less than a minute and you are off back working. If not you get picked up and taken down to the Police station in Saltcoats where I am based, and we can do it there under caution.'

John was bluffing because at that moment he had no probable cause, but he wanted to get it done the easy way.

'I would go all the way to Saltcoats?'

'Yes, that's where I am stationed.'

'Okay then,' Rod said and cooperated, the thought of losing so much of his shift swaying him, much to John's relief.

When Rod left Carol was back on the phone. John stood watching her, admiring her forward facing assets.

When she was free he told her he would be asking the local uniforms to drop in to get DNA tests from the others on the list.

Just at that Carol disconnected her headset and got up to show John the way out. He was surprised to see she was quite thin, not skinny, but not as fat as her chest had indicated. Any normal woman with a chest of the dimension of hers would have a belly to match.

'I think you do a marvellous job,' she said, 'hope I have been a help.'

'Yes, you have.'

He reached out and shook her hand. It was warm and soft to the touch.

'Is it okay if I use the toilet?' he asked her.

'Sure, it's the last door on the left there,' she said as they reached the office door, and she pointed down the corridor.

Carol returned inside her office and John headed to the toilet.

It was surprisingly clean and fresh to the smell. There was a urinal and a cubicle, and he quickly got in the cubicle and shut the door.

He dropped his trousers and boxers. He had to slip them past his penis because it was now full of blood, almost rampant, brought about by imagining getting his head between Carol's lovely fun pillows.

Sitting on the pan he quickly started rubbed himself. He closed his eyes and imagined massaging Carol's globes, getting her nipples hard, imagining her asking him to have sex with her.

Then it was over. He didn't climax but simply lost the lust. He looked down at the limp lump in his hand and felt like crying. It wasn't Karen that failed him like he thought, or probably hoped. No, it was him. His sex drive was letting him down.

He tried reviving it, massaging it and closing his eyes, trying to think more lustful thoughts about Carol but it wasn't working.

As he sat there he thought he heard muffled voices from next door. He quickly sorted his clothing and left the cubicle, listening intently for the voices again. As far as he could make out the building was empty apart from Carol in the office.

The muffled voices were coming from the opposite direction of the office, this was from the room with the with the extra-large padlock on it. He pressed his ear against the mirror that was on the wall but still heard nothing.

John went back to the office and knocked gently again before opening the door and looking in.

Carol was eating a Mars bar. God, he thought, she was even doing that seductively. If he stood there long enough he thought he would be heading back to the cubicle to try again.

'Carol, is there anyone else in the building?'

'No, unless Andrew is in his office although he usually pops his head in here first.'

'What's in the room at the other side of the corridor?'

'Oh, that's where Andrew keeps his antiques. Well, they are his wife's, she has a business in Glasgow. Import and export, something like that.

I have never been in it, strictly confidential,' she said with a smile.

'Okay, thanks for all your help,' John said and closed the door, leaving Carol to her chocolate delight.

John looked at the door into the other half of the taxi's unit. It was secured by 2 large hasps and padlocks. His antiques must be very valuable to be secured like that. He stuck an ear to the door, wondering if he heard noises from within, or if he imagined it. This time there was no noise from inside.

As John walked out of the Kennedy Kab's offices, Andrew Kennedy was just reaching for the door handle and was surprised to see the Policeman leaving his premises.

'Is something wrong, officer?' the business owner asked.

'No, fine, all dealt with.'

'Right,' he said, his curiosity piqued.

John said nothing else and walked past him to his car. He didn't mention about getting the note from the taxi boss.

John left the industrial estate and headed for the Kilmarnock Police station. He hoped D.S. Cairns would help him get the rest of the taxi drivers on the list to get their DNA samples, obviously with the assistance of the local plods.

GAFFNEY AGAIN

John Rose waited until the Friday before visiting Gaffney again. He was sure word would have got back to him from his mates that the other associates of Kennedy from back in 2003 had been DNA tested.

Gary opened the front door with a curt- 'Oh, it's you.'

'All right if I come in?'

'I suppose so.'

They sat where they had a few days previously.

'I'm not taking the test,' Gary said, arms folded across his chest in defiance.

'I don't need you to.'

Gary was surprised and looked at John for an explanation.

'But I thought you wanted me too.'

'I don't need to because I know you did it.'

Gary went to speak but John put a hand up and he let the detective continue.

'It was you and Malcolm Hood that were there that night. I think Malcolm took the blame for the mistake or you grassed him up to save your skin.'

'Wait a minute, I never shopped anyone in my life.'

'Whatever, that's not important now. I am also sure Malcolm was dead before he left the flyover, and it wasn't suicide, but that's the bit I am only guessing. An educated guess but a guess just the same.'

Gary sat quietly. John never spoke either, he waited to hear what Gary would say next. The only noise in the otherwise quiet room was very faint voices from the television that Gary had failed to kill the sound completely.

'If I don't do the DNA you don't have proof. That was if I did it.'

'Gary, there were only 2 people who knew for definite what happened that night. One is dead, the other told me you were there.'

Gary looked at John with hostility in his eyes but didn't say anything.

'It's him I want, Kennedy. You were merely his pawn that night, following orders. In my heart I couldn't put you in prison and leave your son at the mercy of Social Services, he needs his father, but I want Kennedy.'

'So why the visit? Oh, wait a minute, you want something for me.'

John nodded.

'What do you want me to do?'

'I want to know how he makes his money. I am sure he would make a good living from his taxi firm but that wouldn't fund his lavish lifestyle.'

'I still have a few mates who drive for him and keep in touch with them regularly. They keep me up to date with what he is up to.'

John smiled to himself. He felt a bit like the guys on the TV show the A Team, whose catchphrase was- I love it when a plan comes together. He hoped the next thing that came out of Gary's mouth would supply the answer he needed.

'So, what's he up to know?'

'He runs a brothel in Glasgow and is involved in people trafficking to supply the girls. He supplies young girls for other folk too.'

John tried to not look surprised, but this was bigger, much bigger than he thought.

'What paedophile groups?'

'Anybody who has the money. Young virgin girls from Eastern Europe.'

'What do you know about the brothel?'

'Nothing much. Just that it is pretty high class, and a lot of important and well-heeled guys are punters.'

'Are you sure your mates aren't just making this stuff up?'

'No, it's common knowledge among the older guys. To them it's a bit like telling me what I am not involved in because I am Richard's full-time carer.'

'Right, here is what I am going to do. In my report I need to say you took a DNA test. I will get one done by somebody about your age and who has never been in trouble with the Law. In return, I need the address of the brothel.'

'I don't know it, just that it's in Glasgow. How can I get that? My mates aren't daft, they will suspect something if I just ask them.'

'Say it's for yourself. When was the last time you, you know?'

'That's a question. God, it must be over 10 years. I was going with a woman for a while, but she ran a mile when she met Richard. After that I just thought all women would have the same reaction, so I gave up after that.'

'What about his antique collection?'

'Collection? No, his wife has an antique business in Glasgow. She imports stuff from all over Europe.'

'Imports? How?'

'They have a van and a driver. Goes over the Channel once a week collecting antiques from all over. Of course, often there are more than antiques in the back.'

John thought he had discovered Kennedy's way in for his sex slaves.

John then leaned forward and stretched out a hand to Gary.

'Do we have a deal?'

Garry did likewise and they shook on it.

John got up and handed Gary his business card.

'Just get in contact. Any way you want. Phone, email, even a text if you want. I could drop in again, but I am sure if you don't see me again it will be too soon.'

'Okay, and thanks. A lot of coppers would have loved to put me behind bars.'

'Not me. You have lost a lot of your life already. No, as I said, you were a pawn, I want the king, it's your old boss I am after.'

As they walked to the door Gary gently grabbed John's arm.

'You were right, I was there. You know, that night. It was supposed to be a warning to Bremner. Hoody messed up. I didn't know but he had taken drugs that night. Kennedy went ape-shit and wanted us both killed but Hoody fessed up. Kennedy had him killed and had me doing all his shitty work until I was left looking after Richard.'

'Thanks,' John said, then turned and left.

Back in his car, John thought, God, this detective lark is really easy and smiled to himself as he started up his engine.

HOUSE OF ILL-REPUTE

It was the following Monday before John received a text from an unknown number with a Glasgow address on. Nothing else, just a name and address but he knew who it was from.

He had already prepared Karen for the next part of his plan at the weekend by telling her he would be working late backshift one day that week. He told her there was going to be a series of big, hush-hush drugs raid across Ayrshire that needed every spare officer available.

After all, he couldn't put in a report about the alleged brothel without actually visiting it. There again, deep down he also had hidden agendas, personal ones.

For one, he had never been in a house of ill-repute and wondered if they were like they were portrayed on television or films. Secondly, there was his own sexual performance, or lack of it. Could lying with a prostitute cure his apparent impotence? Or was Karen really the root of his problem? After all, he failed to come when he tried having a chug in Kennedy's place.

John quickly checked the address out on his computer, turned out it was in Shawlands area of Glasgow, quite near to the only nightclub in the south side of the city.

Next night he drove to Glasgow. After the Satnav said he had reached his destination he noted the spot then drove on for another couple of streets. As he walked back towards the address it started to rain. Only light drizzle but it meant the few people out and about were hurrying to their destinations, head down and basically ignoring anyone else who was out and about.

Apart from John whose walk was measured, all the time his heart beating a bit faster than usual in anticipation of what lay ahead.

The address was hard to find, the street was full of shops that weren't fond of displaying their street number about their premises. He eventually tracked it down to a non-descript door, the paint faded and a small nameplate on the wall beside saying 'Alison Flowers, registered masseuse.'

For a moment he thought it might be a wind-up, had Gary Gaffney set him up? If he had he would be getting DNA swabbed and he would face his punishment. John went out on a limb for him and wasn't going to be messed about.

Pausing for a moment, he took a breath, opened the door and walked in. The landing was clean and tidy much and much as he would have expected in a building of its age. Nothing to suggest brothel, especially a supposed high class one.

He had only taken a few steps down the close when a big, bald gorilla, dressed all in black, including an expensive looking leather jacket, stepped down from the steps above and into sight.

'You got an appointment?'

'No. I thought you could just turn up.'

The big guy just shook his head. 'Appointments only.'

'How do I get an appointment?'

The guy walked toward him menacingly and put his hand in his pocket. For a second John though he was going for a chib or knuckleduster but he just pulled out a business card and handed him it.

John looked at it, it was a plain card, nothing fancy, and simply said the same as the doorplate, Alison Flowers, registered masseuse and a mobile number.

John took the card and turned to leave. Two things came to mind, he was certainly at the right place, who knew a masseuse who needed a minder and secondly, if Alison was a registered masseuse, where was she registered? John laughed to himself as he thought about that. Probably because of the nerves he was feeling.

John left and headed quickly back to his car. His mobile phone was switched off and placed in the glove compartment. Didn't want to lose it or get it taken off him if the hired hand thought there was something was dodgy about him.

He dialled the mobile number and waited as it rang.

The woman simply repeated the phone number when she answered.

'Is that Alison?' John asked. His throat was suddenly dry, he wished he had brought a bottle of water with him.

'Yes, how can I help?' Her voice seemed very officious, business like.

'I need a massage and wondered if I can book in for one.'

'When for?'

'Tonight, preferably, I am in the area.'

'Ten o'clock. Or is that too early?'

John looked at his watch, it was nearly 20 to 10.

'No, that sounds perfect.'

'Name?'

'John Mullin.'

He stuck with his own first name, his fear being if he used a different first name he could be caught out and gave the second name gave to give it an ironic twist in his mind.

'Okay, sir. See you then.'

'Oh, by the way, how much is it, you know, just for a straight massage?'

As soon as the straight word was out John felt a bit of a div, but there again, what were you supposed to say?

'It's £200 for up to an hour with no extras.'

'Fine, then I will see you then.'

John checked the time on his phone when he hung up. Just under twenty minutes to wait. Right at that moment he could go a drink. He would have loved a stiff one but there was no way he would drink and drive when he was kind of on duty. More like unofficial duty.

The fee seemed a bit hefty to somebody from the sticks, but it did prove it wasn't just a massage he was getting. Fortunately, he'd lifter £300 from the cash-line earlier in the day but he thought he was taking a bigger chunk home than he would now be.

As he had time to spare he checked the streets looking for Kennedy's Roller. If he bumped into him in the knocking shop Andrew was not the type of guy who would think it was just a coincidence him being there. Even after he'd wasted 15 minutes it occurred to him he wouldn't be using a car as noticeable as the Roller around the City. There again the guy's ego would probably make him think he was untouchable, and he wouldn't care who saw him showing off his wealth.

Back at the knocking shop, the same muscle greeted him with the same phrase. 'Got an appointment?'

'Yes, I have now. Mullin, 10 o'clock.'

The leather clad thug spoke into a mike on his wrist. Very professional, John thought.

'Maulling did you say?'

'Mullin.'

John hadn't noticed but Mister Muscles had a small black earpiece in as well.

'Up you go.'

The guy stood back and let John walk up the steps. At the top of the steps there was a fancy looking entrance door, a big contrast to the nondescript front door, that opened as he reached it. Another gorilla stood behind the door as he walked in.

Inside was a lectern and a woman stood behind it. This could be Alison Flowers but John thought not.

'Mister Mullin is it?'

John nodded.

'Take a seat.'

There were 3 chairs with red velvet on the cushions and back, the wood painted gold, faux opulence.

The woman walked round and handed him a book that looked like a menu from a fancy restaurant. She was in her 30's and dressed in a smart business suit. The kind of woman John would probably fancy himself, if he met her under different circumstances.

John opened the fancy booklet it and saw it was the brothel's bill of fare.

'Some of the girls are not on duty tonight,' Alison, or not Alison, informed him.

John nodded and looked through the large glossy pictures, the girls posed more like catwalk models than call girls. Some looked very young to him.

After checking the whole book, he made his pick.

'Karli,' John enquired. She looked older than the others who all seemed like very young teenagers to him.

The woman nodded and walked round to collect the menu.

'Yes, she is available tonight. As I said the fee is £200. Cash or card?'

John realised he missed a trick, paying by card would have given him a traceable link through their bank. Although how would he have explained that to Karen?

'Cash,' he said.

As the woman took his money she gave him the ground rules.

'No kissing, no bareback, no biting, no striking,' she said, then added, 'those are all extras.'

'Okay fine, no extras,' was all John could think to say.

'We will need to give Karli a few minutes to get ready,' the woman said. Then asked, 'what is it you do yourself?'

This almost had John on the back foot as he hadn't prepared a back story.

'I run a whisky distribution company based in Girvan. I am up staying with a friend and his wife here in Glasgow.'

John stopped and looked down at his hands before speaking again.

'My wife died 2 years ago. Cancer. It's been a while.'

There was an awkward silence before "Alison" spoke.

'Not many families miss it. It's a terrible way to die. Oh, she is ready now, room 5.'

KARLI

John walked along the corridor. The doors on the left-hand side were numbered with odd numbers, the doors on the right were evens. Number 5 being the third room along on his left.

He knocked gently on the door, then walked in.

Karli was sitting on a wooden blanket box at the end of the bed and got up when he walked in. She was dressed in a white silky slip and when she stood up John saw she was naked beneath it. She had very small breasts and he saw she had no pubic hair. Her skin was almost porcelain white, and her jet-black hair cut in a bob.

Without speaking she helped him out of his now damp jacket and hung it on a hook behind the door.

John took the rest of his clothes off and sat them in a pile on the blanket box while Karli, took off her slip and lay on the bed.

John lay on the bed beside her. The blood, in anticipation had started rushing towards his penis.

It was helped by the Viagra he swallowed when he parked up earlier. He bought them that afternoon from a chemist shop in Saltcoats, far enough from him home so as not to be recognised.

He had never tried the pills before, but they seemed to be working very well.

Karli leaned down and cupped his balls then gently ran the fingers of one hand up his rapidly stiffening shaft.

Up close and even in the dimmed light of the room Karli looked younger than her picture. John reached a hand over and cupped her delicate little right breast. Although her breast was small the nipple was soon solid to the touch.

John realised Karli hadn't spoken yet. Although he was paying for pleasure he still had a job to do. He wanted to get an idea of where in the World she was from. From her looks he guessed somewhere in East Europe but that was still a huge area.

'Am I hard enough,' he asked.

She merely nodded.

She produced a condom from somewhere and took it from the wrapper before putting it in her mouth and expertly rolling it down his shaft.

John couldn't believe she could do that or how good it felt. The anticipation of the sex almost had him coming there and then. He tried to slow his breathing to contain himself.

Karli lay down on her back.

'Missionary?' she asked but said it as if it was spelled mishionary, giving a hint of her accent. John was sure now she was Eastern European.

John nodded and moved above her. Before entering he needed to salve his conscience, much that it was when he was going to have sex with a prostitute.

'What age are you? Fifteen?'

The girl pointed up.

'Sixteen?'

'One more,' she said.

'Seventeen.'

She nodded. Although John wasn't entirely sure she was telling the truth he felt a bit better about what he was going to do.

He slipped in easily, obviously the girl had lubed herself when she was preparing herself for his visit.

John started slowly, tenderly, but after a few minutes thought he might be unable to finish so built up the speed.

The young girl managed to wrap her legs round him and this pushed him in further and closer to finishing. Two minutes later relief flooded through him as he filled the condom with a huge amount of seed.

The relief felt as important as the sexual gratification he felt.

As he lay above her, getting his breath back the girl looked up at up at him, emotionless.

'Thank you,' he said, then slowly pulled out and rolled over, still trying to slow his heart down.

When his breath was back to near normal he turned and looked toward Karli who lay still looking up at the ceiling.

'That was magic,' John said, smiling at her.

She turned towards him, a detached look on her face.

'Wash up,' she said, pointing to the door in the corner John thought was just a cupboard when he came in.

He got off the bed and walked round, holding his wilting cock and the rubber to ensure it didn't slip off.

Inside the small room was a shelf with a basin full of tepid water with wipes and a towel beside it. Next to it, Karli's make-up, perfumes and lubes.

John slipped off the rubber from his now flaccid cock. He wrapped it in a couple of wipes, he was going to take it with him, not wanting to leave any evidence that he had been there.

When he washed he went through to the bedroom. Karli was still lying on the bed.

'Again?' she asked, still emotionless.

'Sorry?'

'You come to bed, we do it again.'

John's ploy worked, making her speak. There was a definite East European tinge to her voice.

'No. Clean yourself up.'

As she got off the bed she looked at him.

'No good?' she asked, this time there was a genuine disappointed look on her face. Obviously she was afraid there might be a negative report from him, something that her bosses would frown upon.

'No, very good,' John said and smiled, nodding to reinforce his enjoyment.

Karli as she walked slowly past him, a little smile played on her lips.

John thought he must be doing something wrong. Maybe all the other clients made sure they got their money's worth. He didn't have a watch or phone to check the time, but he thought the time must be nearly half-way through.

Left alone, he got dressed and carefully slipped the spent condom and wipes in the back pocket of his trousers then sat on the blanket box to wait on Karli's return.

A few minutes later Karli walked back through wearing the white slip again.

John swallowed hard. This poor girl, little more than a child, had been transported halfway across Europe to be used and abused by sick men.

John's job was to save girls from this exploitation but here he was doing exactly that. Hopefully what he learned that night would salve his conscience.

'Thank you,' was all he could think to say.

The girl looked sadly into his eyes. 'Uratowac mnie,' she replied.

John put both his hands out and took one of her hands in his. He held them gently for a minute then turned and left.

As John walked down the corridor the minder stepped out from where the seats were in the waiting area and barred him from making an early exit.

The woman turned and faced him. 'Everything okay?', she said as she looked up at a clock on the wall above her lectern. It was only 10:33.

'Perfect,' John said.

Just at that a light came on at the desk and the woman nodded to the hired muscle who stepped across and opened the door to let John out.

John realised this was Karli letting them know she was okay, and it was safe to let the client leave.

John walked out to even an even heavier shower of rain. As he hurried down the street, he kept repeating in his mind- Uratowac mnie.

Back in the car he wrote it down on his notebook he had stuffed below the driver's seat.

Next morning John put what he thought Karli had said the previous night, "Uratowac mnee" into Google on his work computer. It brought up a Polish dictionary and it translated to "save me". John swallowed hard when he saw the message he gave him and as he remembered the look in the girls eyes the previous night as he left.

'I will make sure you are saved,' he said to the computer screen.

WALKER

John had all the DNA results back from the lab and unsurprisingly there were no matches. Especially Gary Gaffney's. John had asked his neighbour to do a test for him. He said he was practising how to do the swabbing and Colin was one of those guys who was always willing to help.

Finishing his report, he made an appointment to see D.I. Walker to tell him the disappointing news that he couldn't solve the cold case murders of the Mullin family.

Walker sat at his desk in his immaculately tidy office and waved for John to enter before he knocked on the door.

'Here is the final report, sir. I am sorry but it's bad news, I have run out of new leads in the case. The case boils down to the only evidence we have are 4 cigarette butts with DNA on them.

One of the cigarettes was, I am sure, smoked by a guy called Malcolm Hood. He was a drugs enforcer at the time and its believed he was to blame because he torched the wrong house and took out an innocent family.

It would seem he got the blame and jumped or was pushed off a road parapet into the path of an oncoming lorry a week after the fire.

The other remains unidentified although I had all of Hood's associates from 2003 to take DNA tests. Unless someone comes forward in the future and gives us a name I fear the other killer will never be caught.'

'Well done.'

'Sir?'

'Well, I was told you would get absolutely nowhere with this case, but I stood your corner. You proved me right and your doubters wrong. You have practically solved it and if we ever get a DNA match we will have him.'

'Of course, sir, it was nearly 20 years, the guy could be dead by now.'

'Well, I will need to see what you have to work on next.'

'You are forgetting I stop on Friday for a fortnights holiday.'

'Oh, right, I remember now. Going somewhere nice?'

'Benidorm.'

Walker expression changed to that of disgust. A more common place he couldn't imagine.

John didn't think he could hate his boss any more than he did, but his expression brought his resentment to a new low level. Whether he liked Benidorm or not it was John's choice to go there, not his.

John and Karen loved Benidorm and didn't care what anyone else thought.

'It's my 40th wedding anniversary', John added.

Walker whistled gently. 'Well done. What's that, gold or something?'

'Ruby.'

'Well, enjoy Benidorm and I am sure we will have an interesting case waiting when you get back.'

D.I. HANNAH

Next morning John drove to the Scottish Police headquarters in Govan hoping to meet up with his former boss, Detective Inspector Victoria Hannah. He should have made an appointment but wanted to surprise her.

He reported to the front desk, explained who he was and asked if the D.I. was available. The P.C. on the desk made a call then told John to take a seat.

It was a full 5 minutes before Victoria arrived in the reception area. She was surprised to see who was waiting for her.

'Hello John, is something wrong?'

John and his former boss had a fractious relationship when they worked together at Saltcoats. She looked surprised and didn't seem one bit pleased to see him.

'Quite the reverse,' he said, showing her the file that contained the report he had prepared specially for her, on Andrew Kennedy.

'Best go up to my office.'

As they rode in the lift up to the 3rd floor, the atmosphere still cagey.

'How are things back in Saltcoats then?'

'Good. They have given me my own department covering cold case murders.'

'Right, sounds interesting.'

'It is.'

'Who are you working with?'

'Myself.'

'That will suit you,' she said, a wry smile played on her lips as she said it.

Victoria's office was palatial compared to John's cupboard, but he didn't envy her it.

As it wasn't a social call, Victoria was keen to know the reason for John's visit.

'Well, John, what are you after?'

'Andrew Kennedy. Kennedy Kabs in Kilmarnock. Do you know him?'

'Not personally but I know who he is.'

'I have been doing a cold case inquiry into the murder of the Mullin family in 2003. Do you remember it?'

'The Mullin family?'

'The family of 5 wiped out by a fire in the wheely bin.'

'Right, I remember now. It was national news at the time. I was only on the force a few years then.'

'In the course of the investigation I found out Mister Kennedy wasn't the legitimate businessman he appears to be now at that time. He was a drug dealer. A major one in Kilmarnock as it turned out.

He ordered the hit on a guy who owed a lot of money, well a warning, but his henchmen got the wrong house.

Anyway, it turns out our Mister Kennedy is still up to no good. Nowadays he is into trafficking young girls as sex slaves. He is also running a brothel in the Shawlands area of Glasgow.'

'A brothel.'

'A very high-class brothel.'

Victoria looked surprised by John's revelations.

'I will need to check with Vice, see if they have any intel on it.'

'Oh, it's genuine. I checked it out myself.'

Victoria looked at him to check he was being truthful. His look told her he was.

'Were you inside the premises?' she asked almost hesitantly.

John nodded slightly before quickly carrying on with his intel.

'His wife has an import and export business, trading antiques across Europe. They have a van that makes weekly trips across the channel, and I think this is how he brings the girls into Britain. It will probably be how he launders his cash too.'

'Interesting,' Victoria said.

'Interesting? I thought you would have been delighted at the thought of landing a big fish like this and grabbed it with both hands.'

'If it's genuine.'

'For Christs' sake, do you think I went to all this trouble making this file and taking the time to travel up here just to mess with you? I put a lot of time and effort into this because I want Kennedy to go down.'

Victoria put a hand up. 'I'm sorry, John. I shouldn't have doubted you. Whatever else you are, you are a damn good detective.'

John dropped the file on her desk.

'Do me a favour, nail this bastard,' he said, then got up and left.

BENIDORM

Twelve days into their Anniversary break with Karen and John was at the stage he was ready for home. Everything had been great, the weather, the hotel, the sex, when they managed it although Viagra assisted, but you can get too much of a good thing.

They were sitting outside a café bar along from their hotel having a light lunch and drinks when Karen suddenly got animated.

'Look John. That looks like somewhere in Scotland!'

She was watching the Sky news on a giant television outside the venue that was behind John's back. John had to turn to see what his wife was excited about.

Along the bottom of the screen, it said- EIGHTEEN ARRESTED IN RAID ON A SEX TRAFFICING OPERATION IN STRATHCLYDE.

'Imagine that, practically happening on our doorstep,' Karen said, 'sex trafficking. Can you imagine that?'

'Imagine,' John replied. He was surprised at how quickly they had acted. No doubt they had some information about the sex trafficking, maybe John's report filled in some of the missing bits.

On the screen Victoria Hannah was holding a press conference. The sound was turned down quite low, but the café owners had put subtitles on.

'Acting on information received we carried out raids on 5 premises across Glasgow and Ayrshire today resulting in 18 arrests.'

'I wonder where abouts in Ayrshire it was,' Karen asked.

The film then changed to pictures of the different premises they had raided, including the Kennedy Kabs units and Kennedy's house.

'That looks like Kilmarnock,' John said casually.

'Oh my. Here, is that not the woman Hannah that was your boss? My, she's went on to bigger and better. Just think, that could have been you if you had stuck in.'

Just then, on the screen, the girls from the brothel were being herded into a Police minibus carrying their meagre possessions. Amongst them John clearly saw Karli, head bowed, but now safe from Kennedy's clutches.

'Look at those poor girls. I wonder what will happen to them now,' Karen asked.

'I don't know, but it's better than the life they had I assume.'

'Do you know who I blame?' Karen said, her voice now filled with bitterness.

Before John could speak she carried on with her tirade.

'The men that use those places. What kind of sick man, if you can call them men, lies with those girls? Disgusting.'

'You are right, love.'

'You would never do anything like that would you?'

'Me? No.'

'Not even if, well I died?'

'No, that doesn't bear thinking about.'

Karen patted his hand. 'I know you wouldn't. You aren't that kind of man.'

They drank some more then Karen went on.

'Just think, the holiday's nearly over. Back to the slog on Monday.'

John made a face but didn't comment.

'John why don't you just retire? We would get by on your pension.'

Before John could reply Karen added, 'then you could spend all day with me.'

John felt like telling her she had just answered her own question but simply said- 'Next year. It will come soon enough.'

Follow John Rose's story in- The Tuesday Night Killer

Printed in Great Britain
by Amazon